The Billionaire's Melody

Power, Influence, and the Dark Secrets

Rafael Shamsiev

Table of Contents

Chapter 1:

The Mysterious Disappearance

As Kyle Brenner carefully navigated the small floor space between desks with a piping hot, steaming cup of coffee in each hand, he had to step over a briefcase that Dylan Summers, another reporter, had left lying in the middle of the floor. Dana Anderson almost bumped into him, but he managed to avoid her, and she called a hurried apology over her shoulder as she rushed by. After a year of working for *The Seattle Telegraph*, Kyle was accustomed to the frenetic, chaotic atmosphere. Everyone was always in a hurry, eager for the next story.

Finally, he was able to place one of the coffees on his boss's desk. Samantha King, a brilliant investigative reporter in her thirties—tall, blonde, and pretty in a girl-next-door way—looked up at Kyle and smiled. She accepted the coffee gratefully and waited for him to take his seat across from her and retrieve his notepad from his jacket pocket.

"So, what have you got for me?" Sam asked. This was one of the things Kyle appreciated most about having her as his mentor. She allowed him to come to her with a collection of new story ideas, and then she would pick the one that intrigued her the most. It gave him a chance to put his investigative skills to the test. He was there to learn, and Kyle felt there was no better reporter from whom he could possibly learn.

Looking at his own hurried scribbling, Kyle said, "Unfair labor practices of clothing manufacturers in China exporting their goods worldwide?"

Sam shook her head. "Nope. Everyone is bored to tears with that one already. There isn't a new angle we can explore."

"Okay, what about corruption within the music industry? There's been talk of managers bribing radio stations to give their artists more airtime than they would normally get, thus making them seem like a bigger success than they actually are. Choosing the music the public should like instead of allowing consumers to lead the market. There have also been reports of backup singers, sound technicians, and others being underpaid and overworked."

Sam raised her hand for Kyle to stop. "I get it. That one has potential. But knowing you by now, you always leave the best one for last—the one you actually want me to look into. So, what is it?"

Kyle grinned guiltily. He hadn't realized his tactic had become obvious, but he should have known better than to think he could ever pull one over on Sam. "How about up-and-coming country singer Maxine Wilson going missing after partying with influential record producer Wayland Scott? People in the industry say she couldn't hack it and went home to Oklahoma. Her family claims she never came home, and they haven't seen her. It's been a week since she disappeared."

Sam nodded thoughtfully. "I'm listening."

"Her boyfriend is still here in Seattle, making waves. He insists that something has happened to her and that Wayland is responsible."

"Hmmm... Wayland Scott. Isn't he the one who was arrested for sexual assault a few years ago?" Sam was already typing away at her computer keyboard, probably looking for gossip columns that sometimes got the edges of an actual story right before the mainstream press did.

"Yeah, in 2016. Charges were dropped. There was talk that he settled outside of court with the woman who accused him. But he's been clean ever since." Then, Kyle shrugged. "Or he hasn't been caught since."

After a few minutes, Sam stood up behind her desk and grabbed her coat and briefcase. "Come on, we're going to the last hotel where Maxine partied before she disappeared. She never went back to the motel room she shared with her boyfriend. There was a party hosted by Wayland in the ballroom of the hotel the night Maxine disappeared. I want to see if the police missed anything because they assumed she went back to her hometown."

***

Half an hour later, Kyle was standing nervously in front of the reception desk at the Premiere Hotel. Sam was speaking earnestly to one of the front-desk clerks, explaining about the party and her missing handbag.

"But, Madam, that was a week ago! Surely, you should have come sooner to look for such an important item!" the clerk, an older, stern French gentleman, said this with a frown.

She cast her eyes down, pretending to be embarrassed. "I have other handbags, Monsieur...?" She held her hand out to him.

"Delacour." He held her small hand for a moment and smiled. "I am pleased to make your acquaintance, Madam." Then, he dropped the smile and stood back a little, folding his hands neatly on the desk again. "Unfortunately, the hotel cannot be held responsible for lost items."

"The handbag itself is of no great importance. It's something inside the bag that I'm looking for—a key chain that my Pooky Bear," and she grabbed Kyle by the arm and laid her head on his shoulder, "gave to me. It's not expensive, but it has sentimental value. Could I just look inside your box of lost and found items? If it's not there, then I will accept that it's really lost."

The clerk glanced at Kyle's beet-red face, his much younger appearance, and nodded. Obviously, the clerk had seen it all before and knew how to maintain his composure. "Very well. Follow me." He escorted them to a private office. "I'll bring you the box with items left behind after the party." He smiled kindly at Sam and Kyle. "It actually happens a lot more often than you'd think, and you're not the first person to come and look for their missing items after attending a party here. People usually come sooner, though."

Once he left them alone in the office, Sam turned to Kyle and grinned. "We'll have to work on your acting skills. You almost gave away the game, jumping like that when I touched you."

"Yeah, well..." Kyle tried to think of a clever retort. "I'm not used to being groped by my boss."

Sam laughed. "It's a good thing you didn't listen to your parents and end up on Wall Street then."

Kyle's parents had aspirations for him to become a hedge fund manager like his father, but Kyle had different ideas about his future. He had wanted to be an investigative journalist ever since he saw the movie *Spotlight*, where a group of Boston journalists uncovered abuse within the Catholic Church. It inspired Kyle, and it was what he had wanted to do ever since. It wasn't the only area of his life that had become a disappointment for his parents. The revelation that he was gay had also not endeared him to them. It didn't matter. At 23 years old, he knew exactly who he was and where he wanted to be.

After about another 10 minutes of cooling their heels, the front desk clerk returned, carrying a large brown box in his arms with a date scribbled in black marker on the lid. "There," he said, placing the box down on the table between Sam and Kyle. "You can have a look, and I expect you to be honest and take only what is yours. Someone may still want some of the other things in here."

As soon as he left them, Sam opened the box. "What exactly are we looking for?" Kyle asked. Then, he whistled when he saw some of the box's contents. There were expensive watches, cell phones, shoes, and all kinds of items in there.

Sam took out her phone and handed it to Kyle wordlessly. He looked at the picture she had saved earlier. It was from Maxine Wilson. Kyle guessed it was a paparazzi picture taken outside the hotel when Maxine had stepped out for a cigarette. Maxine was wearing a sparkly dress and shoes with silver sequins dusted on the heels.

"Here it is," Sam said, lifting a handbag out of the box. It was a denim handbag with black lace covering the bottom half. It didn't look expensive. "I'm guessing Maxine got this at some sort of fair or something back in her hometown. She was trying desperately to cling to her roots amidst the sudden burst of fame she experienced here in Seattle. Everything was strange, exciting, and new. She just wanted something with her that reminded her of Oklahoma."

Kyle held the picture of Maxine up to the handbag. Sure enough, there it was in the picture—the same ugly handbag clashing horribly with the girl's dress. "No woman would leave her handbag behind if she was running back home. Or anywhere, for that matter."

Sam nodded. "Yup, you got it. The handbag being here is proof that something happened to her. It's enough proof for me, at least."

She rummaged through the handbag, took Maxine's wallet out, and handed it to Kyle. He checked and saw that Maxine's credit cards, cash, ID, and driver's license were still in there. "We have to get this to the police."

"I have a better idea. The police didn't want to listen. We'll take this to Maxine's boyfriend. I want to interview him anyway."

Getting frustrated, Sam swore under her breath and tipped the contents of Maxine's handbag onto the table. Loose change, lip gloss, chewing gum, and eyeliner—all manner of items that women usually carry around in their handbags spilled onto the table. Some of it rolled off onto the floor. Kyle bent to pick up the items and retrieved a tampon, some change, a packet of Kleenex, and a small notebook.

"Here! Look!" Sam cried out, barely taking note of Kyle bumping his head in surprise at her sudden outburst at the bottom of the table. Standing upright, still rubbing his head, he looked at what Sam held in her hand. It was a business card.

Kyle took it. "Colmbs F. Carrer? The music mogul? Maxine was nowhere near enough of a big deal yet to have had anything to do with him!"

"My thoughts exactly," Sam said with satisfaction. "Look at the back."

There was a name scribbled in pen on the back of the business card. "Who is Persephone?"

"Goddess abducted by Hades, queen of the underworld and the mother of Dionysus," Sam said as she took the card from him and stared thoughtfully at the scribbled name on the back.

Kyle rolled his eyes. "I know my Greek mythology. What I meant was, what does it mean in this context?"

Sam shook her head. "I don't know. But you know that story you pitched to me earlier about unfair labor practices and bribes in the music industry? I think it's a winner. We'll go with that. And I know the ideal person to interview—someone who knows the ins and outs of the music industry very well."

Sam held the business card up so that Kyle could see Carrer's name, etched in gold, sparkling on the front of the royal blue card.

"You're going to interview Colmbs Carrer?!" Kyle said, torn between excitement about the story and nervousness about Sam getting under the skin of such an important, rich, well-connected man.

"No," Sam corrected him. "We are. We're a team, remember?"

Kyle paged through the little notebook he had picked up. "I can tell you that's not Maxine's handwriting," he said, nodding at the business card. He showed some of it to Sam. The notebook was full of song lyrics—obviously, songs that Maxine had been in the process of writing. With a chill, Kyle realized that if Maxine wasn't just missing but dead, then these songs would never be completed.

"I wonder if it's Carrer's? I mean the handwriting on the business card," Sam said, and then she shook her head. "No use speculating. I have to get into a room with the guy so I can see what he's about. It will take some time to arrange the interview. Right now, we can go see if we can find Maxine's boyfriend and return her handbag. Not a peep about the business card or about the connection to Carrer. Not yet."

Chapter 2:

Unlikely Clue

"Well, I'm so glad I could set the record straight, Miss King. The music industry is something that's very close to my heart. Of course it is; I've built an empire out of it." He smiled, flashing perfectly straight, white teeth that must have cost his parents a fortune in orthodontist bills, and splayed his hand out, effectively proving his point with the breathtaking view from his spacious penthouse office window in Seattle.

Below, the uptown Seattle skyline was twinkling prettily in the early evening twilight that was descending slowly on the city.

The entire interview with Carrer was conducted while Sam was sitting at the desk, her legs neatly crossed, a notepad in hand, and a tape recorder placed on the dark wooden surface in front of her. Carrer was pacing up and down in front of his window while they talked. Sometimes, he would stare out the window with his back to her and then only turn his head slightly to look at her when he answered. Other times, he would sit on the window sill, arms folded or leaning back. That's the way he was sitting as they finished up the interview. Sam guessed it was meant to convey a casual feeling of just two friends talking, both to put her at ease and convince her that he was being open and honest with her.

He was the epitome of a successful, handsome, and charming billionaire, and Sam could understand why he had been named one of the top 10 sexiest eligible bachelors of the year in Vogue only a few months before. With his steely blue eyes, strong, dimpled chin, and otherwise dark features, it wasn't difficult to understand why women flocked to Carrer. Still, there was something very off-putting about him. Sam had the distinct impression that his smile was a facade, hiding a shark's predatory thoughts underneath. She pushed these feelings away while conducting the interview. She had to be objective.

Yet, now that the interview was done, the feeling resurfaced, and Sam was faced with a problem. Carrer hadn't given her any reason to doubt his answers. He had been brutally honest about the trappings of the music industry and its shortcomings, and he expressed regret that it wasn't conducted in a way that could benefit everyone.

Carrer seemed to be impressed by Sam. And why shouldn't he be? He was under the impression that he was meeting with a fledgling reporter, cutting her teeth on this story. That's what Tony Prescott, the editor-in-chief at *The Seattle Telegraph*, had led Carrer's press liaison to believe when he had requested the interview.

Tony knew how to tread that line very carefully. He hadn't outright told a lie, and he had just deliberately downplayed Samantha's experience and achievements. Then, she had dressed for the part, electing to wear blue jeans and an inexpensive top and putting her blond hair up in a ponytail for the meeting.

It was unfortunate that the facade depended on Samantha coming to the interview alone. Bringing an assistant would have raised Carrer's suspicion and made him more defensive. So, Kyle wasn't there with her. She had wanted to give him some sit-in experience to see how an interview like this was conducted. She even felt a little guilty about not being able to include him.

Oh, well, she thought with regret. *It's not as if he's never seen me conducting an interview before. And there will be other opportunities for Kyle to gain experience.*

After giving the music mogul a perfunctory smile, Sam leaned forward and switched off the tape recorder. Her disappointment at how mundane the interview had gone and the nagging feeling that she had missed something made her drag her feet a little as Carrer escorted her to the door. Her eye caught something, a few photos on one wall of his office, and Sam's mind raced, trying to find an excuse to be left alone in his office.

"Excuse me," Sam said, turning to Carrer, about to take a calculated risk. "Can you show me how to find the restroom? I'm afraid I drank too much coffee, and it's still a long drive back to my apartment."

Carrer looked at her helplessly and then glanced at his watch. Obviously, he had somewhere important that he needed to be, which conflicted with his desire to be nice to this inquisitive and bright, if somewhat naive, little reporter. In the end, he relented.

"Yes, I happen to have my own private restroom. Come, I'll show you."

He walked back through his office to one of the wooden panels that Sam had suspected were actually doors leading to adjacent rooms. The door Carrer opened for her led into a beautifully decorated bathroom, complete with a huge shower. Sam guessed the tiles had been specially imported from Italy.

At the door, Carrer turned to Sam apologetically. "Unfortunately, I have somewhere urgent I need to be. I'll let my assistant know you're in here so she won't lock you inside for the whole night. When you are done, she'll call for someone to escort you to your car."

"Thank you, Mister Carrer. It was a pleasure to meet you."

Carrer took Sam's offered hand and then, amazingly, brought it to his lips and placed a gentle, chaste kiss on the back of it. Thousands of other women would have found the gesture charming, even endearing, but the sandpapery feel of his dry lips on the skin of her hand made Sam's skin crawl.

Sam nodded and was thankful when Carrer let go of her hand. She stepped into the restroom, and with the door at her back, she counted slowly until 15 before she opened the door carefully. Peeking into the office, she saw that it was now empty.

Sam closed the bathroom door behind her and looked around longingly at the rest of the office. In one corner, there was a bookcase and some filing cabinets that she might have wanted to look through. There was also Carrer's computer, which was switched off and looking all too tempting. Yet she knew that the assistant wouldn't give her enough time alone in the office to dig around, and the last thing that Sam wanted was to be caught red-handed snooping through Carrer's personal things. Sam wasn't some mastermind hacker, and she was certain that Carrer's PC would be password-protected.

Besides, the point was rather moot. If there were anything incriminating in his office, Carrer wouldn't have risked it by leaving Sam alone in there. Either there was nothing to find, or it was locked up, and Carrer knew that Sam wouldn't be able to find it.

Instead, she walked over to the back wall of Carrer's office behind his desk. There was a huge painting depicting some sort of abstract artist's work that Sam had no doubt must have cost a fortune.

It wasn't the painting that had caught Sam's eye, but the many pictures hung there, all of them important people standing next to Carrer. Some of the most important artists that Carrer's company, *New Seattle Sound Unlimited*, represented were standing next to Carrer in these photos. There were also a few of Carrer with other celebrities, most notably Oprah Winfrey and Jared Leto. The photo that Sam had wanted a closer look at was of Carrer standing in front of a nightclub with an older gentleman in his late fifties. The other gentleman, a tall, very thin, scarecrow-like man, was dressed in an expensive Armani suit and looked rich and powerful as well as disturbingly familiar. Looking at his face, Sam tried to remember who this guy was.

She was about to give up and turn away when it suddenly clicked into place. Feeling as if she had just stumbled onto something huge, Sam turned back to the photo to make sure. With a hand shaking from excitement, Sam took out her phone and opened the camera app. Then, she took a photo of the framed picture where Carrer was standing with his arm slung companionably around the shoulder of none other than Christoph Berger, a computer software magnate from Austria, who settled in the States some years ago to build a film company. Berger's whole empire came tumbling down when his gruesome and highly illegal extracurricular activities came to light. After an investigation that took years, it came out that Christoph was using his film company to lure underage girls, kidnap them, and sell them to influential men in Saudi Arabia, Taiwan, Portugal, Greece, and all over Europe as sex slaves.

At that moment, Christoph Berger was incarcerated, serving 25 years to life on over 30 counts of kidnapping, rape, child molestation, and a whole shopping list of other charges. These days, Berger was something like a leper, and any association with him was cause for suspicion. In the weeks and months after his arrest and the lead-up to his well-publicized trial, Berger assured the public that he wasn't the only influential and powerful man connected to this *worldwide sex traffic ring* and that he would be exchanging the names of some of these men in favor of a deal. No such deal was struck. It was widely speculated that Berger was threatened to stay silent and was now quietly serving his time, afraid for his life, terrified of the very people who he had once upon a time called his friends and associates.

Why in the world would Carrer keep this photo on his wall? Sam thought. Any sane person would have removed it just because of the stigma attached to Berger these days. Even if Carrer was just a naive but loyal friend, convinced of Berger's innocence, it still would have been better for him to remove the picture from his wall. Instead, he kept it there, as if he just didn't care what people thought.

Maybe it goes deeper than that, Sam's mind whispered to her as she stepped away from the photo and walked to the door of Carrer's office to let herself out. *Maybe he knows*; *maybe he just doesn't think there's anything wrong with what Berger did.* After sensing that predatory glimmer behind Carrer's eyes, Sam thought her last speculation was probably close to the truth.

Sam drove back to the office. She could have gone home, but she was way too keyed up. She knew at least one person would be burning the midnight oil. Just as she suspected, the light in Tony's office was still burning. After knocking politely and hearing Tony grumble something unintelligible from inside, Sam let herself in.

Tony was standing behind his desk, a cigarette clamped between his thick lips. He was scowling at his desk as if he had misplaced something and was wondering where it had gone. A short, round guy of nearly 60, he looked like a cross between Danny DeVito and Jonah Jameson, Peter Parker's boss in the Spider-Man comics.

As Sam took a seat in front of his desk, she pointed at Tony's head. "Glasses up top, boss."

Tony looked surprised and reached up, finding that his misplaced glasses were indeed on top of his head. He scowled and put them on, then finally looked at Sam and burst out laughing. "Well, look at you! Miss high school newspaper reporter!"

Sitting down and leaning back in his chair, he crushed the cigarette in the overflowing ashtray.

"I'm surprised they haven't fired you yet," Sam remarked drily. "The '80s called, boss. They want their health hazards in public places back."

Refusing to be baited by Sam's cheek, Tony patiently waited for her to tell him what she had found out—what had her so worked up. Sam gave him a rundown of the interview, then took out her phone and showed him the photo she had taken in Carrer's office. In the background, the nightclub's name was clearly visible in pink neon. It was called *Persephone*. Sam knew in her gut that this was what the business card in Maxine's purse had referred to. She finally had her clue to link Maxine to Carrer.

Tony looked at Sam with eyes sparkling with excitement—the same excitement that all reporters worth their salt felt when the chase for the story was on.

"You have the go-ahead to dig as deep as you want. Just be careful, kid. This guy Carrer and men like him have all the resources in the world and everything to lose."

Chapter 3:

Beneath the Glitz

Sam shifted around uncomfortably, trying to pull the tight, black miniskirt down so it would show a little less. With the short skirt, a tight white blouse, and fishnet stockings showcasing her lovely legs, Sam actually looked fantastic, but she wasn't used to wearing outfits like this particular one. At least the smart black jacket, which was part of the ensemble, made her feel less naked.

"Stop fidgeting," Ryan said, scowling at Sam. "If you're going to go unnoticed at that place, you have to resign yourself to the fact that you're going to be wearing this." He was trying to fit Sam with a tiny camera poking out between her cleavage. "There. Now it will be able to record what you see."

After a few days of digging, Sam and Kyle had found the very glitzy, super-exclusive nightclub *Persephone* that Carrer owned. The only problem was that the entrance was by invitation only. They did, however, employ cocktail waitresses from one particular company. Samantha and Kyle had approached one of the waitresses. Mary Jacobs had been way too scared to say anything about what went on in the club, but in the end, she agreed to switch places with Sam for a few hours.

Sam was the same build as Mary, and with a black wig covering her blond hair, she hoped to blend in as the waitress. Hopefully, the dim lights of the club would allow the switch between them to go undetected.

That had left Samantha and Kyle with the predicament of figuring out how to record footage inside the club. That's where Kyle's partner, Ryan, came in. He owned a fledgling tech security company. He had been able to come up with a solution in the form of a little camera to be fitted to Sam so she could move around freely while recording what she saw. The camera's footage would be grainy, and the sound wouldn't be perfect, but it was better than nothing.

They were waiting in a car in the alleyway adjacent to the club. It was dark, and the dumpsters nearby smelled to high heaven. By 9:30 p.m., exactly on cue, the side door leading from the kitchen in the club opened, and Mary stepped out to have a cigarette. The door was supposed to stay locked, but Mary had informed them that it was an open secret that the door could be opened from the inside so the staff could nip out for a cigarette when they wanted to.

"Most of the others vape," Mary had said to Sam. "I'm one of the few who still smokes old-school cigarettes. I've tried everything to quit. Maybe if I don't have to work there anymore, I won't be so nervous all the time."

As they watched the ember from Mary's cigarette bobbing up and down in the dark—she was approaching the dumpsters—the camera over the nightclub's door picked up her movement and followed her progress down the alley.

Sam opened the passenger door of the car, and Mary slipped inside. Then, she handed her cigarette and security pass to Sam. Wrinkling her nose a little, Sam took it, and she and Mary switched places. Now, Sam stuck her hand, the one holding the cigarette out, and flicked the half-smoked cigarette onto the alley's floor. She stepped out of the car, then turned back and leaned inside as if saying goodnight to whoever was in the car. Hopefully, the security footage of the club will show a girl quickly greeting her boyfriend during her shift.

Sam walked up to the back door. She took out the security card and swiped it at the panel for access. There was a clicking sound, and she opened the door. The bustling kitchen greeted her. She gave the car a last look and waved, then she stepped inside. As Sam's eyes adjusted to the bright kitchen in front of her, the door shut behind her. She was in.

"Hey, waitress girl! Over here!" Sam looked, and one of the cooks was pointing at a tray filled with cocktails. Food usually wasn't served at nightclubs, but then, this wasn't your standard run-of-the-mill club. Sam stepped over and picked up the tray. Years working at a coffee shop during her time studying at Harvard Law had at least prepared her for this. She already knew where to take it. Mary was the regular waitress at table number 12, where Carrer brought and often entertained business associates. That was why Mary had been the perfect waitress for Sam to impersonate.

Pushing open the club doors, the stifling darkness and strobe lights overhead mixed with the loud music to create an atmosphere that enveloped Sam. She squinted her eyes and scanned the room, trying to figure out which of the silver tables set against the wall on the far end of the club floor was the one she was supposed to take the drinks to.

Then, she saw him, Colmbs Carrer, dressed in an expensive black suit and silver tie, sitting at one of the tables. He was surrounded by a group of men, and they were chatting and laughing together. Sam took a quick mental note of the other men. There were four in total, and she recognized two of them: One was Wayland Scott, the record producer associated with Maxine's disappearance. The other man was Ivan Berger, Christoph's younger brother and newly appointed CEO of Berger Pictures since Christoph's incarceration.

Following her discovery of Carrer's connection to the Bergers, Sam had done her homework so that now she recognized the younger brother. Still, she was surprised to see him there, not because she believed the fairytale that he spun to the media that he had nothing to do with his brother's sex trafficking but because the company had taken such a huge hit and Sam had expected Ivan to learn from his brother's mistakes and be more careful about his illegal dealings.

Her eyes flicked to the last two men sitting at the table. They were dressed in the traditional clothes Sam associated with men from Saudi Arabia. Sam guessed that they were probably important clients.

Bracing herself and taking a deep breath, Sam took the stairs at the side of the dancefloor and walked across the raised platform to the table. As she put the drinks down, not knowing who had ordered what, the men hardly glanced at her. Wayland picked up the drinks and placed them in front of the correct man. Then, he leaned back in his chair to get a good glance at Sam's behind, as she was still leaning over the table. She felt herself flush but, at the same time, tried to linger in that position because the conversation she was picking up was interesting.

"So, the merchandise is safe?" one of the Arab men was asking.

"You mean besides a bit of smudged makeup and a swollen lip?" Carrer laughed. "She's otherwise undamaged. Ready to be sent. You just need to sort it out with your guy at customs. She'll be added to the other stock you've ordered. I believe that puts us at 6 units, at $30,000 a head."

The cavalier attitude they had when discussing the women as if it were just business as usual made Sam's stomach turn. Obviously, they weren't in the least bit nervous about discussing it here. They barely used code for what they were doing!

"What about the boyfriend? I understand he is still making trouble." The second Arab man seemed not as eager as his friend to be assured that all was well. Sam felt her heart flutter. They were talking about Maxine Wilson! Sam was sure of it.

"We're handling it," Wayland piped up, once more leaning forward. "It's not for you to worry about."

Sam picked up the empty plates where the men had enjoyed snacks and deliberately knocked over Wayland Scott's drink. She wanted to buy more time and have an excuse to continue listening to their conversation. The men hardly noticed. Only Wayland grabbed her by the elbow. He turned Sam around to look at him.

"You better fetch me another drink, hon." His fingers were digging into the soft skin of her arm. Sam nodded meekly and kept her eyes averted.

She picked up the broken pieces of glass and wiped up the spill with a few napkins.

Wayland left her to clean up, picked up a manila envelope from the table, and handed it to one of the Arab gentlemen. "I have another potential product that just came in this morning. Fresh off the bus from Texas. Seventeen-year-old runaway. She showed up at my offices with a guitar under her arm. Can you believe it?"

The Arab man took what Sam assumed was a headshot of the girl in question out of the envelope. He stared at it for a minute, then said, "I'll try to find a buyer and get back to you."

"Sure. I can have her record a single. Have it play on a few small radio stations to buy us some time."

Sam knew that she should get going, at least get Wayland's drink. She couldn't hang around at their table without looking suspicious. She would have loved to stay to hear more, but if Carrer looked up and really looked at her, he would possibly recognize her as the reporter who had interviewed him a week before. However, Sam didn't think he would recognize her. Men like Carrer rarely took note of the people who served them, and a young reporter he had sent away without any helpful information would become completely forgettable to a man like him.

Still, she couldn't afford to risk it. She turned around with the tray now stacked with plates and other rubbish from their table, including the pieces of broken glass.

As she walked a few paces, she heard Wayland say to the others, "That waitress, she's not the girl that usually serves our table. And she was way too interested in the conversation."

"Well, who do you think she is?" This was from Carrer.

Sam suppressed the urge to start running, but she did walk back straight to the kitchen. Setting the full tray down on a random counter, she walked to the back door. Fumbling with the security card, Sam finally unlocked the door and was out. Behind her, she heard one of the cooks in the kitchen calling after her, swearing.

Sam sprinted to the car and jumped inside. "I don't think it's safe for you to go back there just now," she told a frightened Mary as Ryan pressed down on the accelerator and the car sped away.

Kyle, sitting in the passenger seat next to Ryan, turned to look at Sam. "What happened? What did you find out?"

Sam knew they would be watching the video she had recorded as soon as they got back to Ryan and Kyle's place. For better or worse, Mary was going with them. They had better figure out what to do with her because, after tonight, she might be in danger if she tried to go back.

"They were talking about trafficking girls right in front of me. They didn't even try to hide it."

"Well, that's great! It means you got exactly what you wanted, isn't it?" Kyle saw the freaked-out expression on Sam's face and realized there was more.

"They talked about shipping Maxine out soon! They referenced her boyfriend, so I knew it was her they were talking about. But I just started on this story! There's no way I'll be able to stop them from sending her out of the country!"

Kyle thought he understood. If they had started investigating this a year earlier, they may have been in time to save Maxine. As it was, they were still working at the edges of it. Knowing that Maxine Wilson's fate will haunt all of them.

"They talked about another girl. A seventeen-year-old girl that Wayland Scott showed pictures of to one of the brokers. He said he'd talk to his client and get back to Wayland soon. That means that somewhere out there, there's a seventeen-year-old runaway from Texas in danger of becoming the next target, and I have no idea yet how to stop that from happening to her."

Chapter 4:

Shattered Dreams

Parking in the driveway of the charming little house in Madison Park, Sam was wondering if Chloe Wilcox had changed her mind about the interview. After tracking her down, it took Sam and her team more than a week of repeated emails and phone calls to convince Chloe that her story needed to be told.

Kyle rang the doorbell, and then they waited. Sam had time enough to get worried before the door was opened by a pretty brunette who looked suspiciously out at them before opening the door. Chloe was twenty-two years old and lived with her older sister. The two of them bought the house together after Chloe turned twenty-one and got her inheritance. Both their parents died in a car accident seven years ago.

She took them through to the living room, where she sat across from Sam, nervously fidgeting with the sleeve of her oversized hoodie. She was still a pretty young woman, but it was clear that the trauma of the past few years had finally taken its toll. She wasn't wearing any makeup. Her hair was done up in a messy bun. It looked dirty and oily, and Sam suspected it hadn't been washed in some time. Her chipped blue nail polish didn't hide the fact that her fingernails were bitten down to the quick. A thick hoodie on such a warm day led Sam to believe she was trying to hide something. Sam wondered if Chloe had been self-harming and didn't want them to see the cuts on her arms.

According to Chloe's emails, she's been in therapy since just after her parents' accident. She spent some time in a wellness clinic for substance abuse a few months before.

As Kyle set up the recording equipment, Sam tried to put Chloe at ease. "As I've explained, we'll only record your voice. You won't be shown on the camera at all. If you need someone here with you, that's okay, too. What about your sister? Will it be better for you to talk while she's here?"

Chloe looked at Sam with those haunted eyes of hers. Her fingers went into her mouth, and she started biting the skin on the sides of her fingertips. Sam felt a phantom sympathy pain in her own hand; the skin on Chloe's fingernails was already raw from being bitten and torn off. She placed her hand back in her lap and shook her head.

"No, I don't think I'll be able to tell you everything if she's sitting here. And I know I should. At least once."

"You never told the police what happened to you?" Sam asked this carefully. She didn't want

Chloe to feel like she was judging her for not going to the police. So many cases of abuse go unreported because the victims fear not being believed.

Chloe shook her head again. "I told my sister some of the things, and that's it."

Sam looked over at Kyle, and he nodded, indicating that everything was ready. Turning back to Chloe, Sam said, "If you feel uncomfortable about Kyle being here, then please don't hesitate to tell us."

Again, Chloe shifted uncomfortably. "No, it's okay."

"Okay, Chloe. In your own words, just tell us how you met Colmbs Carrer. You were introduced to him by Wayland Scott?"

Chloe nodded. "Yeah. It was after I finished recording my first demo. Wayland said it was going to be huge. He treated me like I was already a star, booked photo shoots, and everything. He said we needed to get ahead on publicity so my face could be plastered on every billboard and in every magazine. He took me shopping and introduced me to loads of people in the industry. I didn't really know at times if I was coming or going."

"How old were you when you recorded the demo?"

"It was just before my seventeenth birthday. My parents had been dead for almost two years by then."

"So, there was more than one photo shoot?" Sam had already known some of it—how Wayland had gotten compromising pictures of Chloe to blackmail her with later.

"There were three photo shoots. The first two were just normal. I had done some modeling when I was about thirteen or fourteen years old, so I already knew the drill."

"Tell me about the last photo shoot."

Chloe hugged herself tightly. "Wayland took me to his place. We had already partied there a few times with other people, so I didn't think it was weird. I thought it was a little weird when I saw that there weren't any other people there. But Wayland... I sometimes forgot he was a much older guy. Anyway, he gave me a drink. It was something strong, like whiskey or something. I think he drugged me because, after a while, I started feeling all floaty, like I was walking on a fluffy cloud."

Sam wanted her to continue before Chloe lost her nerve, so she pushed her a little. "What happened then?"

"The photographer showed up. I didn't know who he was at the time, but later, I learned his name was Emilio Florez. His photos often appear in fashion magazines. He's as old as Wayland. They're friends."

"So, you never met Florez before that moment?"

Chloe shook her head. Then, realizing that she needed to speak because they were only recording her voice, she leaned forward slightly to speak into the recorder. "No, I only met Florez that day. It was in September, so three months before my seventeenth birthday."

"Was Florez the one who brought the coke?"

"Yes. It was the first time Wayland offered me drugs. He had given me alcohol plenty of times before then. He asked if I wanted to try it. Florez even joked that I was too young and that they could get in trouble for giving me some. Wayland said I could try some if I promised not to tell anybody. I was curious, so I tried it."

"Did you know at the time that Florez was taking pictures of you while you sniffed coke?"

Chloe sighed and looked away, embarrassed. "Yes. I think because of the stuff Wayland gave me earlier, I didn't care. I thought I was being cool or whatever."

Chloe rubbed at her face, and as she did, the sleeve of her hoodie pulled up, and Sam could see the scars on her arms. She only got a quick glimpse.

"We can take a break if you want," Kyle told Chloe. Sam looked at him and saw the worried expression on his face. He was reacting to seeing the cuts on her arms.

"No, it's okay. I'd rather get it over with."

She took a deep breath and then continued, "Florez took a few pictures and then started to undress me. We were in a bedroom. I don't know if it was Wayland's bedroom or just a guest room. He kept telling me how beautiful I was and how I was going to be a star. He took naked pictures of me."

Now tears were running down Chloe's face. Sam handed her a Kleenex, and she wiped them away.

"Florez put the camera on a tripod and set it up so it would keep taking pictures. He came to the bed. Things were a little hazy at that point because I don't know when he took his clothes off, but he was naked when he came to lie next to me on the bed."

"Where was Wayland when this was happening?"

"He was standing next to the tripod. He had his pants off, and he was touching himself, watching Florez touch me. I asked him to stop and told him I felt sick, and he just said he'd make me feel better. He had sex with me. It wasn't weird or anything. Not later, like with Carrer."

"While Florez was having sex with you, did Wayland do anything else?"

Chloe nodded. "He took the camera off the tripod and started taking pictures himself. He walked around the bed and was telling Florez what to do. I passed out once or twice, and every time I came to, it was still happening."

She burst into tears then, holding her face in her hands. Sam quietly went over and sat next to her, patting Chloe on the back. "I'm sorry that happened to you, Chloe. You are so brave, speaking about it now."

Chloe shook her head. "If I was brave, I would have gone to the cops then, right after. Wayland dropped me off at home as if nothing happened, and I tried to forget it."

"You didn't tell anyone else what happened to you?"

"No. I was too ashamed. I was scared because of the coke and because I knew that he had those pictures of me."

Sam stood up and went back to her seat.

"Did you ever ask Wayland about the pictures or bring up the incident?"

"No. He treated me as if nothing happened. I tried to forget it. I told myself it was just sex, and it wasn't as if I was a virgin before, but I kept remembering passing out, and Florez just kept on going. I remember asking him to stop more than once, and he ignored me. I tried to tell myself, maybe I only thought I told him to stop in my head, that maybe he didn't know that I didn't want it to happen."

"How long after this incident did Wayland take you to meet Carrer?"

"It was three weeks later. He called me into his office and asked me if I was on my period. No guy had ever spoken to me like that before, and I was shocked and embarrassed. I said it was none of his business."

"And what did he say to that?"

"He told me that the pictures he had of me made it his business. I told him I wasn't, and he said he was going to pick me up for a party. He told me I should dress in something sexy. I didn't want to go, but he told me he had those pictures of me. I realized that I didn't have a choice."

Sam handed Chloe a bottle of water. She took a few sips and wanted to give it back, but Sam told her to keep it and sent Kyle to fetch them some more water from the car.

"He drove me to Carrer's house. We met Carrer at the front door, and Carrer told Wayland to wait in the study. Then, Carrer took me by the hand up to a bedroom. The pictures Florez had taken of me, some of them were blown up and hanging on the walls. All the things Florez did to me... you couldn't see his face, only mine. I started crying, and Carrer told me to keep going. He sat down on the bed and started undressing himself, all while watching me cry."

Chloe's hands were shaking, and Sam honestly didn't know if she would be able to tell her all of it.

She ended up telling them some of it. She wasn't drugged at that time, and she remembered everything Carrer did to her. He was into inflicting pain, and he tied her up and beat her with a belt before raping her.

Afterward, when Wayland drove Chloe home, he told her that $2,000 would be paid into her account, and she should take her money and buy herself something nice. He told her that Carrer was the big boss and that he hadn't seen much potential in Chloe as a singer.

"I haven't been able to sing since it happened," Chloe told them, tears streaming down her face once more. "At one stage, while I was tied up, Carrer told me to sing. He told me if I was good enough, then he wouldn't hit me with the belt. I sang to him, and then he did what he did. While he was hitting me, he called me his songbird."

Chapter 5:

Dark Dealings Revealed

After the interview with Chloe Wilcox, Sam was out for blood. Preferably, she wanted to see both Carrer's and Wayland's heads roll for what they had done to that girl. Not to mention Florez, the sleazy photographer.

The age of consent in Washington was 16 years. That was one of the reasons why Chloe and her sister never went to the police when the truth of what happened to Chloe came out. People hear the statistics, and they think that they don't have a case if they were older than 16 when it happened.

What they didn't realize was that there's a caveat attached to that specific law, which states that if the person in question is younger than eighteen, then their partner can't be more than five years older. At the time when that happened to Chloe, she was seventeen years old, and both Wayland and Florez were already in their thirties. So was Carrer. That meant that Chloe definitely had a case, even if she couldn't prove it was rape. Sam thought that even them being charged with statutory rape would be more justice than Chloe ever got.

She told Chloe this but asked if she would hold off on going to the police until they finished gathering evidence. Her case would also be stronger if Sam could find other witnesses.

"It may take as long as a year, maybe less, maybe longer," Sam told Chloe. She wanted to be as open and honest with her as possible.

Chloe wasn't sure that she even wanted to go to the police or testify at all. She was scared, and after what Sam thought had happened to Maxine Wilson, she was right to be. If it became known that Sam was digging into this story, then Chloe would become a liability for Carrer. Unfinished business, a loose end that needed tying up.

So, Sam was under extra pressure to do her digging in secret so that Carrer and the rest of them didn't become aware of what she was doing until it was too late.

Shortly after the interview, Sam could have strangled all of the men with her bare hands. She wasn't about to do that, though. She hadn't come so far in her career by being reckless and giving in to every emotion.

So, Sam practiced caution, and with Kyle's help, they found three more girls in a matter of weeks who had similar stories to tell. This proved a pattern of behavior of rape, torture, and threats that was very disturbing, but it still wasn't enough because Maxine Wilson was still missing, and nobody had an inkling of where she was or what had really happened to her.

Thinking that if there was Maxine, there were bound to be others, Sam started digging into the pasts of all three men. She cross-referenced all three reports of missing girls. What came up was startling. Since Carrer first started his company fifteen years ago, there have been over twenty girls that went missing that were connected to either Carrer's company or that of Wayland Scott or Emilio Florez.

The girls were all young, aspiring singers or models. They had different levels of talent, but they had all been beautiful and younger than 18.

Over 20 girls, and nobody had connected the dots yet? It seemed shocking until Sam pulled up a few statistics. In Washington, D.C., around 2,200 girls went missing every year. There were a number of reasons. Some of them were runaways, and some of them were trying to escape a terrible family situation. And some of them were indeed lured away by sex traffickers.

The girls they found, who were connected to one of the three men, were most often runaways, who came to Seattle hoping to pursue a modeling career or a recording contract. In three of the girls' cases, Emilio Florez had been in direct contact with each of them before they disappeared. He had told police that he had been scouting for fresh talent, and the girls' modeling portfolios had been passed to him through talent agencies.

His messages and emails to the girls were all professional and above reproach. It backed up his story that he was offering them a chance at a career in modeling if they could come to Seattle. Covering his ass, he had even told them to bring a parent along with them.

Once the girls set foot in Washington, they disappeared, and Florez maintained that he had never actually met with any of them. Sam gleaned all this from the missing person's reports filed by the girls' parents. She had a trustworthy contact who got her this information, one that she knew wouldn't raise red flags with the three men. Sam's contact worked in the police's filing department, and she handed Sam the reports.

Five of the other missing girls were connected to Wayland Scott, but the basic elements were the same. In his case, the girls were aspiring singers who, according to Wayland, never made it to their first audition.

In six other cases, the missing girls were not reported missing by their parents but by a schoolteacher when they hadn't shown up for school in a few weeks. In those cases, the girls really were runaways, trying desperately to escape terrible family situations, physical and emotional abuse, sometimes sexual abuse, alcoholic parents, or parents who were drug addicts.

As the stark reality of this story started to set in for both of them, Kyle and Sam realized it may be a lot bigger than just the three men. If the girls were being trafficked, there was a good chance that the modeling agencies that had forwarded Florez the information about the girls were in on it. Did he pay them to send him information on potential victims? Victims who may be written off by police as just runaway teens from troubled homes?

Through some digging, Kyle discovered the location of four women who were still reported missing in their home states but never returned home after meeting with Carrer. These were the ones Sam was most interested in interviewing, but only one of the girls agreed to see her. Mary Chase told a similar story to what Chloe had already told them: the pain Carrer liked to inflict, the humiliation, and the rape. Later, there were threats that she was to keep quiet and money paid into her account, presumably by Carrer.

Mary was a straight A student from a stable home who just happened to have aspirations of becoming a singer. Unlike Maxine, she had a much better support structure that she could have fallen back on had she returned home. Unfortunately, she was 25 years old then and had never told her parents what had happened to her.

As far as her parents were concerned, she was still missing.

Sam couldn't understand it at first. There were no pictures of drug use or compromising sexual photos that Carrer could have used against Mary. So, he paid her off instead. The young woman told Sam that she felt too ashamed at first to return to her parents because she knew what her going missing had done to them. In a sense, she felt like she deserved what had happened because she had gone to Seattle against their wishes.

Now, years later, she thought that her parents were better off not knowing the truth. She never finished school. She took Carrer's money, was still taking his money, and tried to build a life for herself in Seattle. A life that involved working at a restaurant as a dishwasher and living in a tiny apartment with a guy who was clearly much older and looked like a drug-using, laid-back musician.

The amount Carrer was paying in exchange for her silence was enough to cover her rent and buy food for both her and her partner. For a man like Carrer, though, it was chump change. Carrer and Mary had agreed to these monthly payments rather than a lump sum payment. Sam guessed that Carrer wanted to ensure Mary's silence and wasn't sure she would keep quiet if she spent all the money in a few short years. Hearing that Carrer was still paying her off gave Sam some hope. *Follow the money*. That saying was often used when trying to prove someone's guilt where bribery was involved.

Sam contacted a U.S.-based research firm that had launched a database with tens of thousands of relevant pieces of information on companies from data sources around the world, including many about corporations. Sam was specifically searching for the public financial records of *New Seattle Sound Unlimited*. It was there—everything from offshore accounts, tax records, litigation records, and property transactions. Sam was taken aback by the sheer volume of information available. Luckily, she didn't have to sift through them alone.

Kyle helped a great deal, and so did his partner, Ryan, though Sam reminded Ryan that he would be working for free since she couldn't really afford to employ him permanently.

On Tuesday evening, after bribing the two men with a sushi dinner from their favorite restaurant, they were in Sam's apartment working late on the story.

Sipping on her wine, Sam could feel her eyes getting grainy and very tired. She was about to call it a night when Kyle suddenly yelled, "I've got him!"

Kyle showed Sam Carrer's company employment records. He had found the transactions they were looking for: the money paid to Mary to keep her quiet. On the company's financial records, she was marked as a remote–freelance employee. This meant she was supposedly working from home but wasn't permanently employed. Kyle found amounts that matched that one and managed to link them to all the women who were still reported missing but were, in fact, not missing at all. Sam realized that was why the rest of them had all refused to speak to her. They were afraid they were going to lose the money, but also that their lives were in danger if they didn't keep quiet.

This was a huge breakthrough. Sam was hopeful that, if a bit of pressure were put on them, the women would break their pact of silence and talk to her about Carrer, especially if she could confront them and tell them she knew they were being paid for their silence.

Sam was suddenly wide awake, excited by the adrenaline dump in her system. That's when her cell phone rang. She answered it without looking at the name displayed on the screen. As soon as Sam heard the sounds the person on the other end of the line was making, her whole body froze.

Someone was crying hysterically, begging for her life. Sam knew that voice. She had been editing the footage, almost constantly listening to that woman's voice as she told her story. The screaming woman on the other end of the phone was Chloe Wilcox.

Sam was panicking, only partially aware that Ryan and Kyle were standing in front of her, frantically asking what was wrong. She was lost in the sound of Chloe's suffering, sure that she was being murdered because she had dared to tell the truth about Carrer's abuse. Sam was forced to listen to Chloe's screams until the very end.

When it was over and Chloe's voice was silenced, Sam could only imagine what had happened as she fell to her knees on the carpet of her living room. Tears were streaming down Sam's face. She still had the phone clutched tightly to her ear.

"See what happens to little songbirds when they can't keep quiet?" She felt a chill running down her spine. It was Carrer's voice. Of course, after what he would see as Chloe's betrayal, he would want to kill her himself. He was a sadist and had enjoyed her pain.

Now he was enjoying hearing Sam's.

"You would do well to remember this moment, Miss King."

And just like that, he was gone.

Chapter 6:

Cat and Mouse

"The police are not doing anything. I don't even know where to start looking for her body." Chloe's sister, Jenny, was furiously wiping her leaking eyes with a Kleenex. Sam sat across from her, feeling the guilt eating away at her stomach.

It's been three days since Sam got the call from Carrer and heard Chloe screaming on the other end of the line. Sam was sure Chloe was dead. She had told Jenny of her certainty. At that point, Chloe had been missing for four days.

Sam had given her statement to the police. They told her the call had come from a burner cell phone, impossible to trace. Without a body and no evidence that Chloe was actually missing, the police couldn't even take Carrer in for questioning.

One of the policemen had gone so far as to tell Sam that if she wanted to ruin the reputation of such a powerful man, a man who was a stand-up guy in the community, who often donated to charity, and whose reputation for being a devout Christian was public record, then she better have more proof than just claiming she heard him murder a random drug addict over the phone.

Sam realized that as irritating and unfair as this statement was, it was accurate. There would be no justice for Chloe, Mary, Maxine, or any others until she had all the story elements and could present all the facts. This made Sam more determined than ever to dig under the surface of Carrer's musical empire and to expose all the worms wriggling around in the rotting flesh underneath it.

She had to dig up all the buried bodies, both metaphorically and literally, and she knew it wasn't going to be easy. It was going to be dangerous.

Driving back home after she visited Jenny Wilcox, Sam spotted a suspicious car in her rearview mirror. Maybe she was getting paranoid, but she was sure she had seen the same car following her on her way to Jenny's house. It was an older blue sedan, and Sam thought she recognized the scraped paint on the car's nose.

To test this, she deliberately took a right, then another right, and a left. Each time she checked, the car was still behind her. It hung back, allowing other cars to get in the space between them, but each time Sam took a random turn, the car was right there.

Drumming her fingers on the steering wheel, Sam wondered what to do. She was on her way to see Kyle and Ryan. She didn't want to lead the person following her to their apartment, and she especially didn't want the person tailing her to know where she was going after that.

An idea dawned on Sam, and she pulled into the parking lot of a department store. She saw the other car park behind her, a few spaces down from her car. The driver of the suspicious car was just a dark figure sitting quietly, watching her car intently. Taking her phone out, she quickly typed a message and waited for a reply. Sam's contact replied to her text almost immediately.

Taking her handbag from the passenger seat, Sam hopped out and locked the car with a click of her remote; then, she headed into the department store. She took a makeup case out of her handbag as she walked and pretended to apply some lipstick, using the mirror to watch the stalker. She saw an older, nondescript man with grey hair and a brown jacket step out of the car. He was walking slowly, following Sam inside but not being too obvious about it.

Sam took out her cell phone again and typed a short description of the man to her contact. Then, she headed into a clothing store. Picking a few items of clothing at random, Sam headed to the changing rooms.

Pacing up and down inside the small cubicle, she nearly jumped out of her skin when her phone started ringing loudly. *Shit!* she thought, *I should have put it on silent.* She answered her phone with a shaking hand.

"I'm here," the female voice said on the other end of the line. She was talking softly. "What store are you in?"

Sam quickly explained where she was waiting, and soon enough, there was a knock on the stall door. Sam opened the door, and a harried-looking Dana Anderson stepped inside. Dana was another reporter who worked with Sam at *The Seattle Telegraph*. Dana usually worked on political stories. She was a plain-faced, serious woman with short, greying hair and strange green eyes. She looked somewhat like a soccer mom, plain and unassuming. It belied the fact that Dana was an excellent reporter with a sharp mind and a no-nonsense attitude.

She handed Sam the oversized handbag she was carrying. Sam pulled out the items she had requested. She put the dark wig over her blond hair and stood still as Dana helped her straighten it. Then, she put on the sunglasses and the red coat and finally helped Dana put very bright red lipstick on her.

When she was satisfied, she turned back to Dana. Holding up her hand, Dana said, "I don't want to know. Whatever it is you're working on, just be careful, girlie. You may be in above your head." Sam nodded and thanked her for bringing the stuff to her so quickly. Dana smirked and waved it away. "You're just lucky my oldest daughter is an up-and-coming Broadway actress."

Promising to go and see her daughter's next performance, Sam squeezed Dana's hand.

"Your friend is hanging out in the food court, watching the store. Let me know when you are safe."

Sam nodded and closed the stall door behind her as she left. She slung the bright red handbag that Dana had brought as part of Sam's new costume over her shoulder. Sam walked right past the man in the brown jacket. He glanced at her; her outfit was that eye-catching, and he just as quickly dismissed her.

Sam had learned the trick in a spy movie. If you want to go unnoticed, a loud outfit is the best disguise because if people are looking at your clothes, they are not paying attention to your face.

She knew she'd have to send someone for her car later. She had no idea if it was just the one guy she had already spotted who was tailing her. With his kind of resources, Carrer could employ a whole bunch of people to follow her and watch her every move. She knew now that she wouldn't feel safe in her apartment while she was busy with the story. Chances were good that Kyle and Ryan were no longer safe either.

Luckily, Sam knew of a place they could hide out. On the outskirts of Medina, her father had a holiday house that he had left for Sam when he passed away some years ago. It was all she had left of her father, who had been an insufferable bastard and an incurable womanizer. Sam hadn't really wanted anything from her father, whom she hadn't spoken to since he walked out on his family when she was six years old. The holiday house was worth a pretty penny and was still technically in her father's name. Sam doubted if anyone knew of its connection to her. It would make the perfect base for operating moving forward.

As Sam climbed into the Uber, she glanced back at the department store. The guy who was supposed to be following her hadn't come out yet. He thought she was still in the changing rooms of the clothing store.

She knew it wouldn't last long. She got the Uber driver to drop her off at Kyle's apartment building.

Sam rang the bell nervously. When Kyle opened the door, he was taken aback by her appearance. She stepped inside, giving them a quick rundown of what had happened. "Jesus, Sam!" Kyle was looking pale. This, along with the call where Sam heard Chloe being murdered by Carrer, was freaking Kyle out.

“Yeah, I know. Which is why I’ll completely understand if you guys want out.” She looked seriously at both of them.

“Don’t be ridiculous,” Ryan said matter-of-factly, and he came to hand Sam the bugs she had requested. “Just be careful when you’re planting these. If you get caught...”

Sam gave the guys detailed instructions on how to safely reach her father’s house and told them to follow them to the letter. They promised to meet her there later and take every precaution to make sure they were not being followed when they left the apartment.

Leaving their apartment, Sam got into another Uber to take her to *K-Rex Entertainment,* Wayland Scott’s recording company. She walked up to the receptionist and showed her email correspondence between Wayland and herself, or at least the alias she was using, Olivia Marx. The email was real. Sam had reached out to Wayland, pretending to be an aspiring singer. After seeing photos that Ryan had doctored of Sam and running a few actual photos of a 17-year-old Sam through a program to change it somewhat, Wayland had agreed to *Olivia* coming in for an audition.

Sam had zero interest in actually auditioning. She knew the gig would be up as soon as Wayland laid eyes on her and realized she wasn’t who or what she had pretended to be. Wayland's assistant was too polite to mention anything about the clear age difference between the photos she had of Olivia Marx on her system and the woman now standing in front of her. Instead, she treated Sam with icy politeness, asking her to wait while she made a call. Sam went and took a seat in the chairs in front of the receptionist's desk.

Coming here, Sam knew that Wayland wouldn't be available. Ryan had hacked into Wayland's assistant's computer system and made sure he would be out of the office.

The assistant gave Sam an annoyed glance as her hand stretched out to the phone, presumably to call Wayland to inform him that Olivia Marx—a very older-looking Olivia Marx—was there at the office waiting for him.

The phone rang before the assistant could pick it up. She stared at it for a second or two and then picked up the receiver. "You've reached the office of Mr. Scott at K-Rex. It's Louise speaking. How may I be of service?"

Louise listened for a moment and then interrupted the person on the other end of the line. "Well, for Pete's sake! That's why we have the equipment in the first place. How on earth did you get the job working at the front desk in the first place if you don't know how to sound an alarm!" She listened some more and then scoffed, "Sure,

I'll be right down. I obviously don't have anything better to do!" She put the receiver down and pasted a little smile on her face before turning to Sam.

"I'm sorry, but it seems like there's a fire in one of the offices, and the incompetent person working at the front desk has no idea how to sound the fire alarm. I'll have to go down and do it myself. Mr. Scott isn't here and will only be back tomorrow. I'll have him give you a call when he's ready to see you, okay?"

"Of course. No problem." Sam stood up and walked out of the office. Next door, there was a cleaning supply closet that she slipped quickly into. She left it a crack open and watched as Wayland's assistant left the office to go downstairs.

Once the assistant was outside, Sam slipped quickly into Wayland's office. Following Ryan's instructions on how to plant the bugs, she hid one in a potted plant and the other one underneath a ceramic elephant statue.

Then, she stuck the third one behind a portrait. Just as the fire alarm started warbling from above, Sam hurried out of the office. On her way out of the main building, she blended in easily with the stream of people leaving the building.

She was smiling because Kyle's call to Wayland's assistant had been a stroke of genius. Now, they would be able to listen to Wayland's meetings and perhaps find the girl who Wayland was targeting as the next victim.

Chapter 7:

Whistleblowers and Witnesses

Sam sat in the coffee shop, waiting for the mystery contact to arrive. She had no idea who she was meeting, so naturally, it made her nervous.

The meeting had been set up by Kyle. The person had reached out to Kyle anonymously several days ago by sending hand-delivered letters to *The Telegraph*'s offices. Kyle had stayed in contact with the letter sender, utilizing the sort of cloak-and-dagger techniques that one often saw in cheap spy thrillers.

The irony was that those techniques often worked precisely because no one took them seriously.

Kyle had taken out ads in the wanted section of the newspaper, writing messages in code under the Writerboyy113. The contact wanted to meet Sam in the coffee shop but didn't want her to know beforehand who she was meeting. It was all very frustrating for Sam.

"If they really have information that they want to share with me, why don't they just contact me themselves?" Sam had asked when Kyle suggested that she meet with the contact.

"Maybe because they know you have a massive target painted on your back and wouldn't take it seriously? Aren't you suddenly getting hundreds of fake tips weekly?"

It was true. Ever since Carrer found out that Sam was onto him, she had been receiving a number of false tips that she had to follow up on and rule out. Sam guessed that Carrer wanted her to be so busy investigating these that she didn't have time to chase down any real information. He also wanted her to dismiss any real tips that came in, in the same sense that someone who keeps crying wolf will be dismissed after a while.

For the last week and a half, Sam, Kyle, and Ryan were living at Sam's father's place in Medina. When they had to leave the house, they used disguises, different cars, and sometimes Ubers and taxis so as not to be spotted. In the offices of *The Seattle Telegraph*, they were safe. Anywhere else, all bets were off.

Sam tried not to draw too much attention to herself by fidgeting, but it was difficult. She felt impatient and keyed up, and sitting still like this made her feel exposed and vulnerable.

The bugs she had planted in Wayland's office weren't delivering any crucial information yet. Sam had no idea who the girl that Wayland was targeting was. She was afraid that the bugs would be discovered before they found the girl, and they would just end up reading about her in the paper as another runaway teen who mysteriously disappeared.

All they could do at that point was listen to the recordings, try to make a list of Wayland's contacts, and identify people involved in the operation who might bend under pressure and tell them the truth about Wayland and Carrer's illegal dealings.

"Um, excuse me, is that seat taken?"

Sam looked up as she heard the timid voice. She recognized the question as the one the contact and Kyle had agreed on. The person standing beside Sam's table was a young man in his late twenties who had the buttoned-up and nervous look of either an accountant or a computer tech. Sam hoped it was Carrer's accountant. That would make her job so much easier because he would know all about the dirty money coming in and going out.

"No, please," Sam said, and she gestured to the empty chair. "I'm dining alone. It seems I've been stood up."

The young man nodded and sat down opposite Sam.

He leaned forward and held out his hand. Sam shook with him, and then, putting her hand under the table so he wouldn't see it, she wiped it clean. He was sweating profusely, and Sam was a little disgusted by the slick feel of his palm brushing against hers when their hands had touched.

"Pierre Travis. That's my real name." He looked around nervously.

"Just relax, Pierre. The more nervous you look, the more attention you're drawing to yourself."

Sam sat back and smiled as the waitress approached to refill her coffee cup and take Pierre's order. When she was gone, Pierre leaned forward again.

"You don't understand. If they find out I've been talking, they'll kill me."

"Hey, now, look at me." Sam tried to talk as calmly as possible. "They're already after me. Now, let's start from the beginning. Who are you, and how do you know Colmbs Carrer and Wayland Scott?"

"He's my father," Pierre said, as if Sam should know what the hell he was talking about.

"Who? Carrer?" That would be a scoop all by itself if she was interested in writing a gossip column. She had no idea that Carrer had a son, and given the research she had done on Carrer, she didn't think many other people knew either. It wasn't a matter of public record.

"Yeah. He got my mother pregnant and paid her to keep it quiet. My mother was seventeen years old at the time. I guess you could say she was one of his earliest victims."

Sam nodded. "And he doesn't know you or have a relationship with you?"

Pierre shook his head. "He has no idea I'm the son he doesn't want to think about. When I started working for him, I hoped to find some dirt on him, something I could destroy him with. Now, I'm so scared for my own life. I need help."

"So you work for *New Seattle Sound Unlimited*?" Sam was taking notes as they spoke.

Pierre shook his head. "No. And you won't find anything there. Carrer keeps that business of his as clean and far removed from his other business as possible. I mostly work at *Persephone*. It's a nightclub. I'm an accountant, so I handle the books."

Sam felt her heart leap in excitement. If Pierre could get his hands on actual records of dark dealings and hush money, then that would be a fantastic bit of evidence. She didn't want Pierre to notice how excited she was.

Instead, she sat back and let him tell his own story. Sam listened as he told her about money coming in for a *product* purchased through Persephone. At first, Pierre thought he was handling the money for a drug operation. That, along with shipments where he had to transfer money to cover bribes paid to people at customs, made Pierre believe he finally had the dirt on Carrer that he had been looking for. He had the address of a shipment yard and the container number where the product Carrer was shipping overseas was stored.

Playing the amateur sleuth, Pierre had gone there and tried to take pictures with his camera phone. He had watched the shipping container from the shadows and noticed armed guards standing watch over it. “I saw someone approach. It was Heather, Carrer’s assistant. They seemed to be delivering food to the guards, but then I saw the guards opening the container, and a girl, a teenager, had come running out. She was caught by the guards, slapped, and forced back into the container. The guards took the bags of food and water from Heather, and she left soon after that.”

Pierre had realized that it wasn’t a drug operation he had evidence of, but human trafficking. That changed the whole game for him. “I knew if I gave the meager evidence I had to the police, then a few people would be arrested, and Carrer would take a financial hit, but the operation would just keep on functioning. I needed someone like you to blow the whole thing open.”

“I’ll need you to keep on working for Carrer so you can feed me information while you do. I’ll also need the address of the shipping yard, the container information, and anything you can get me to help expose this operation."

"I can get you anything you want as long as you promise to actually expose him. There was another reporter a year ago who tried writing the same story. In the end, he was paid off by Carrer to keep quiet. Can't say I blame him. Carrer almost ruined his life before he agreed to take the hush money."

"Who is this reporter? I'll need a name."

"Dylan Summers. I think he also works for *The Seattle Telegraph*."

Sam could feel the color draining from her face. Not only did she know Dylan Summers personally, but they had worked together on other stories. He was a veteran investigative journalist and used to be something of a mentor to Sam. Until now, she always thought he was one of the best, most honest reporters she knew.

"There's one important person you should speak to. Timothy Brooke. He used to be a friend of Carrer's."

"You mean Timothy Brooke, the country singer who stepped away from the whole music scene a year ago?"

Pierre was nodding. "They had a huge fight. It happened at the club. Carrer introduced Timothy to his overseas clients and other associates. I think Carrer wanted to bring Timothy in on the operation. They grew up together, so they've known each other for years. When Timothy realized what Carrer was involved in, he was horrified. He didn't want to throw Carrer under the bus, but he wanted nothing to do with him after that. He stepped away from it all rather than help Carrer or turn a blind eye."

"What makes you think he'll cooperate with me? He didn't turn Carrer in when he found out. He's probably still loyal to Carrer."

"Timothy's life went to shit these last few months. He spent time in rehab. I can give you the address of the place he lives now, completely off the grid."

Sam took the details from Pierre. After that, he said he needed to go. Sam stood up with him. "This goes without saying, but please be careful. I really need the information you can give me. I need someone close to Carrer who can tell me what he's planning, but I don't want you to get killed because of it. One of the girls that Carrer raped and tortured went missing shortly after I interviewed her. I heard Carrer kill her over the phone. Her body is still missing."

Pierre nodded. "Trust me, I know exactly what the stakes are, but you're the one that Carrer wants to see dead at the moment. So, please take your own advice, Miss King, and watch your back."

Chapter 8:

Network of Silence

Watching the video footage of her interview with Timothy Brooke, Sam wondered how the public was going to react to it. Timothy, or Big Tim, as he insisted everyone call him, came across as a pompous jerk.

He was a key witness, though. The information he had given Sam had been insightful, and Sam knew she couldn't cherry-pick what to show at the end of the day. The public deserved to hear the whole story.

Big Tim had been candid about his friendship with Carrer, telling Sam about the wild drug-fueled parties both at Persephone and at Carrer's estate in Broadmoor. "It got rough," Tim had stated. Words that still left a chill on the back of her spine. "There were prostitutes that Carrer paid, and he had to pay extra because he liked getting rough with them. It was all consensual, though."

Tim had told Sam about the meeting Carrer had set up, trying to bring Tim in on the deal he had with clients in the Middle East and Europe. When Tim realized they were talking about kidnapping and selling girls, he was horrified.

Sam watched herself ask the difficult question to Big Tim, "If you were so outraged and knew more girls would be kidnapped and sold as sex slaves, why didn't you go to the police?"

Here, for the very first time, Timothy actually looked like something resembling a human being. "Cowardice is what it was Miss, pure and simple. I knew what Carrer was capable of. I thought if I sacrificed everything I had worked for, it could somehow buy me absolution from the whole thing, and I could sleep at night. If I wasn't involved, then I'm innocent, right? The truth is, not a day goes by when I don't think of the girls that Carrer and Wayland have access to. Like you, I've been connecting the dots. I've seen a pattern, and I know that some of them are in foreign countries being subjected to god-awful things, all because I was too much of a coward to speak against Carrer."

He started crying then, so Sam had a few minutes of footage of the big, broad-shouldered man crying into a Kleenex. Sam thought that the last bit was important and had to stay in. That last bit may endear Timothy to the public after all.

A message alert on her phone drew Sam's attention away from her computer screen. It was from Pierre. He had something to give to her. For the meeting, Sam donned a wig and took one of the cheap cars she had been forced to buy so

Carrer's people couldn't tail her as she moved around in public, investigating the story.

Pierre was already sitting at their usual table when Sam arrived. As soon as she sat down, he pushed a brown envelope across the table. "Don't open it here!" he hissed as if she was new to all this and just about to. She suppressed the urge to roll her eyes and put the envelope down on top of her handbag, out of sight. "It's proof of the transactions I told you about."

Pierre had identified transactions of hush money Carrer had paid to a cabinet member of transport, Louise Sutton. Hearing this and finally having the paperwork to prove it made Sam wonder how far Carrer's influence really stretched. Was the minister of transport in on it? Sam had enough to warrant an interview with Louise Sutton, at the very least. She was curious to hear what Sutton would have to say and how she could possibly justify taking hush money from Carrer to expedite paperwork and look the other way as shipments of girls kept in containers left U.S. waters to be transported to the Middle East, Asia, and Europe as sex slaves.

"Thank you for this," Sam said, and she meant it. Over the last few weeks, she has grown quite fond of Pierre. The risks to his own safety he was taking in order to give her the information for her story wasn't lost on her. Pierre was becoming her friend despite his naturally nervous disposition.

He was a lot braver than he seemed, and Sam admired him for it.

They moved the conversation on to trivialities, but soon, Pierre had to go. They said their goodbyes, and she watched as he pulled his hoodie over his head again before exiting the coffee shop. It was raining outside, coming down in buckets, and Pierre didn't have an umbrella.

The waitress came over to pour Sam a refill. She was just about to take a sip when she heard tires squealing, followed by a crash. Then, she heard excited voices and someone shouting.

The waitress glanced at the windows of the coffee shop. "Did someone get into an accident?"

Sam grabbed her handbag and the envelope and rushed outside. It wasn't difficult to see where the accident had happened because a crowd was already gathering around. Some of them, Sam saw with disgust, were taking pictures.

Sam walked up and pushed through the crowd. Her breath caught in her throat as she saw the crumpled figure lying in the street. It was Pierre.

Sam rushed over. Other people had bent over him, but when they moved away, Sam saw the blood that was pooling around his head and his lifeless, staring eyes. One guy was talking to emergency services, and Sam was glad they were being called, but she knew it was actually a waste of time. Pierre was dead.

"What happened?" Sam asked one ashen-faced guy standing around.

The guy shook his head but then said in a shaky voice, "Somebody, some guy, grabbed him by his hoodie and pushed him into the road. The car that hit him sped off. Do you think they were working together?" He looked over at Pierre's body. "Who was he anyway?"

After telling the guy to make sure he waited for the police to give a statement, Sam knew she had to get out of there. There was no doubt in her mind that it was Carrer's people who killed Pierre. She had no idea how Carrer found out about their meetings, but he had.

Walking back to her car, she felt numb. Every person she passed, Sam wondered if they looked suspicious or if they glanced at her for too long. She knew she was being paranoid, but it felt like there were eyes everywhere, watching her and judging her every move.

She got in her beat-up old car and drove away. She drove blindly without really looking where she was going.

Before she knew it, she was pulling up in front of *The Seattle Telegraph* building. Sam had no patience at that moment to wait for the elevator, so she took the stairs two at a time. By the time she reached the floor of the investigative journalism section, she was panting and sweaty.

She brushed her hair out of her eyes and pushed the double doors open. The bustling open-plan newsroom greeted her. A few people looked up at her, and taking note of the black wig and punk rocker getup that wasn't her normal style at all, they did a sort of double take. Some of them greeted her in passing, but Sam didn't answer. She was a woman on a mission.

Sam took the folder that Pierre had handed to her and slapped it down on Dylan Summers' desk. Dylan looked up at her wide-eyed. "You knew, you bastard!"

For once, the office went completely silent. People stared open-mouthed in shock at Sam, screaming into the face of the veteran reporter.

"You knew about the missing girls, the raped and abused girls! You knew about Wayland's and Florez's involvement! My God, Dylan! For eight months, you knew about Stutton's involvement and the money she was taking from Carrer, and you buried it all! What did you do with the money Carrer paid you to bury one of the biggest stories this paper has ever seen? Did you buy a holiday home? A sports car that you have to keep in the garage because you're too ashamed to drive anywhere? You should be ashamed! You damn well should be!"

"Sam! Dylan! In my office right now!"

Sam turned and saw Tony Prescott standing there with his hands on his considerable hips. He was looking pissed off. "And the rest of you, get back to work!"

Sam didn't turn around to look at Dylan. She marched straight to Tony's office and sat down in front of the boss's desk with her arms folded angrily across her chest. After a few minutes, Dylan came in and took the chair next to her. He sat quietly, refusing to look Sam in the eye.

Tony slammed his door shut and came to sit down behind his desk. He turned to Sam. He was looking at her as if she had finally lost her mind. After what she had seen a few minutes ago, Sam certainly felt a little crazy.

"What the hell are you on about? Screaming at Summers like that for the whole world to hear. Have you gone mad? That's not how we do things around here!"

Sam turned to Dylan expectantly. When he continued to stare off into the distance, Sam spoke up, "Well? Are you going to tell him, or should I?"

Dylan just shook his head. Sam turned back to Tony.

"I recently found out that the story I'm working on, the one about Carrer and what I now know for a fact, is a human trafficking ring, that I'm not the first reporter to get wind of it. Dylan had all the information eight months ago, and he buried it."

Tony frowned, and the color of his face darkened. "That's a very serious accusation to make, Sam. Who told you this?"

"Pierre Travis, who happens to be Carrer's child, was conceived by a woman who was sixteen years old at the time. Carrer has been paying her a large sum of money to keep quiet. Pierre is the accountant at Persephone, Carrer's nightclub, where he does most of his deals with overseas clients looking to purchase an underaged girl for wealthy men in Asia, the Middle East, and Europe. This afternoon, after handing me evidence of an important cabinet member of transport receiving hush money from Carrer, Pierre was run down in the street. He's dead."

"So, you took this Travis guy at his word?" Tony sounded incredulous. He knew it wasn't like Sam at all. She always checked her facts and double-checked them.

"It's true," Dylan said quietly. "What Sam is saying is all true."

Tony stared at Dylan for a full minute before finally finding his voice. "My God, why? Was it the money? Did he threaten you?"

Dylan shook his head. "I didn't take a damn cent from Carrer." He turned to Sam, his eyes pleading for her to understand. "It's not me they threatened, but Rosie. I was hot on Carrer's trail when I got a call from my son one afternoon. Rosie was missing from school. She was supposed to take the bus, but I guess someone came by and picked her up. I just knew Carrer had something to do with it. I got a call from Carrer, reminding me that there were lots of pedos willing to pay top dollar for a pretty girl like Rosie. I promised him that I would drop it, and someone dropped Rosie off here. She was babbling about the nice man who had taken her to the park. She was still carrying an ice cream."

It was starting to make sense to Sam. Dylan Summers had exactly one photo on his desk: that of a pretty, smiling six-year-old girl. Summers fawned over that girl and would tell anyone who would listen how perfect his granddaughter was. Sam felt a little bad about her accusation that Dylan had taken money from Carrer. It seemed that Carrer knew exactly where to hit Summers to cause the most damage and to scare him into keeping his mouth shut.

Then, Sam thought about Chloe, Maxine, and all the other girls. They had been someone's daughters and someone's granddaughters, too. She said as much to Summers.

“Dammit, I know! When Maxine Wilson went missing, who do you think it was that fed your boy Kyle all the information to get you interested in the story?”

Sam scoffed, “You could have just told me.”

Dylan shook his head. “If Carrer found out, he would have kept his promise. I had Rosie to think about.”

Dylan gave Kyle the story because he knew how hard Sam would go after it. But that wasn’t the only reason Sam was the one Dylan had chosen to pass the story on to. Sam didn’t have any living relatives, and she worked too hard to have any close friends.

When it came to levers, there weren’t many in Sam’s personal life that Carrer could pull to get his way.

Chapter 9:

The Double Agent

After confronting Louise Sutton about her involvement in Carrer's human trafficking operation, things blew up. More people got wind of the story that Sam was pursuing. Her life had become a circus of covert maneuvers to avoid Carrer's people and convince others to step forward to give evidence against Carrer and his associates. In some circles, Sam became a leper, and people avoided her on principle, going only by the gossip they heard of why Samantha King wanted to bring down an important, well-loved, influential man like Carrer, who was an upstanding member of the community.

The inevitable rumors that Sam had been romantically involved with Carrer and was now bitter when it ended seemed to be the favorite one to spread. When asked about it, Carrer didn't deny it but gave such an ambiguous answer that people were left to believe the worst of Sam.

She didn't care. She had expected this to happen sooner or later and knew that most of those people would change their tune once she released the whole story.

The Seattle Telegraph had gotten more than a few threats, but Tony assured Sam that they were used to it and would weather the storm. Sam knew that everyone was under pressure because of her, especially Kyle and Ryan, who had to give up their nice apartment in order to live with her in her father's holiday home. Neither of the men could see their respective families or friends because it was just too dangerous.

Luckily, they both understood the importance of what Sam was doing and knew the danger to their lives would end once the guilty parties were arrested. In order to make it happen, they had to continue with the investigation and expose the whole truth.

One Wednesday morning, when Sam was headed out, she got a call from Tony Prescott.

"Hey Tony, I'm just about to get into my car. One of the girls who was paid off by Carrer agreed to see me, so I'm meeting her in half an hour."

"Yeah, kid, you may want to reschedule with her because there's someone here who says he needs to see you urgently, and considering who this person is, I thought you might want to hear what he has to say."

Sam frowned. It wasn't like Tony to be so frustratingly vague. "Well? Who is it? It took me forever to convince this girl to talk. If I try to reschedule, she may decide never to come forward."

"It's Emilio Florez. I don't know if you had time to pick up a paper today, but Vogue, Chanel, and Cartier have all cut ties with Florez following a press statement where both K-Rex Entertainment and New Seattle Sound Unlimited said they would no longer be using Florez as the photographer for any of their advertisement campaigns. They didn't give a reason why they were dropping him, but I think they're setting him up as a scapegoat for the abuse of the girls."

"Jeezus... that's..." Sam wasn't usually so inarticulate, but she was shocked. K-Rex and New Seattle Sound belonged to Wayland Scott and Colmbs Carrer, respectively. For both of them to betray Florez like that meant his career as a photographer was done. It wasn't that Sam put it past both men to throw someone under the bus like that, but Florez was part of their inner circle. He knew where at least some of the bodies were buried, so Sam couldn't imagine why Carrer and Wayland would want to piss Florez off to the point where he would turn to her.

Were they really that worried about Sam's journalistic abilities? She knew that Tony was right. She had to speak to Florez. On the other hand, Florez was now desperate. He might not realize it, being used to people falling all over themselves to speak to him, but his desperation meant Sam had the upper hand.

"Screw it. He can wait. If he's still there this afternoon, then I'll know he's serious about wanting to speak to me about Carrer and Wayland. I think he may have gone there hoping to give me the least amount of information to save his career. Making him wait will show him I'll not be settling for peanuts."

Tony spluttered for a bit and then started laughing. "Have I ever told you you have the biggest gonads of any woman I've ever met?"

"At least once a week," Sam said drily, but she was smiling as she made her way to the apartment of the girl who had finally decided to tell her her story.

Lilly Smith had a very similar story to the one Sam had already heard from Chloe. It was no wonder because the two girls had been friends. What happened to Chloe had happened to Lilly a year earlier, and Lilly told Sam how guilty she was feeling for not warning Chloe against Wayland and Carrer. Chloe's mysterious disappearance was what finally drove Lilly to seek justice for herself and the others.

When interviewing Lilly, Sam paid special attention to her encounter with Florez, making sure she asked Lilly if he knew how old she was when it happened, if he saw Wayland drugging her, and other details that would be damning for Florez when the paper finally would run Sam's story.

As usual, when confronted with their depravity, Sam was filled with an impotent, blazing rage. She wanted to hurt the men responsible but knew she couldn't, not until she had all her ducks in a row.

It was while still feeling the vengeful burning in her gut that Sam sat across from Emilio Florez later. He had been waiting for more than two hours at that point. Sam looked at the man, handsome in a desperately trying-to-hold-on-to-my-youth sort of way; he obviously took great pains with his image, how he styled his hair, and how he dressed. He was arrogant and very preoccupied with his public image.

He was also furious at Sam for making him wait.

"You know how many newspapers would pay top dollar for my story, Missy? I didn't realize the so-called reporters of this rag were so unprofessional!"

They were sitting in the boardroom, the only private place in the building where Sam could talk to Florez aside from Tony's office. The boardroom was called the fishbowl because of the glass doors where anybody looking in could see what was happening. A lot of the people milling about in the office were openly looking over, curious to know what Sam's meeting with this peacock of a man, who had been silently brooding in Tony's office all morning, was all about.

Sam didn't answer Florez. Instead, she leaned over and casually took the video recorder out of her handbag. She had already taken the video back to the part she wanted Florez to hear, anticipating that the meeting would kick off exactly like it had and knowing she would need something to take him down a few notches.

Sam pressed play, and immediately, Lilly's distressed voice, explaining exactly how Florez had raped her, echoed in the room, bouncing off the glass and wood. In this section of the video, Lilly called Florez by name and mentioned his body, how he looked, how he smelled, everything.

Sam watched the color drain from Florez's face and wondered if he was going to throw up. From the corner of her eye, she saw the people outside the boardroom, her colleagues, drop all pretense at minding their own business. They were openly rubbernecking now, and Sam was grimly pleased, knowing Florez was noticing this, too.

When Sam stopped the video, Florez sat like he had been carved from stone. "You bitch!" he finally hissed through his teeth, spittle flying.

Sam laughed. “Sticks and stones, Mister Florez. Now, if you still feel like going to a different paper with your half-baked attempt at saving your reputation while you’re still a free man, be my guest.” Sam pointed at the door.

When Florez didn’t immediately jump up, she took it as a sign that she could continue. “If, on the other hand, you are willing to change your motivations and actually want to help me repair some of the damage you’ve caused, then stay. Tell me everything that you, Carrer, and Wayland did to those girls and the ones who have gone missing. I want to know everything. You’ll be arrested when the story breaks; there’s no use lying to you about that. But depending on how forthcoming you are, I’ll at least be able to tell the police you cooperated with me, and you can get a judge to show you a modicum of lenience. That is the offer; take it or leave it.”

Sam sat back in the chair and patiently waited for Florez to think about her offer. At one point, Kyle came in and brought both of them coffee and biscuits. When Kyle left, he glanced at Sam and gave her a thumbs-up behind Florez’s back. Sam suppressed the urge to smile back.

Finally, after another few minutes of giving her the silent treatment, Florez nodded. “Very well. I’ll give you a moment to get your recorder ready. You’re going to want to record exactly what I have to tell you.”

After Florez left, promising Sam that he would meet her again the following day to go over more details, she felt emotionally drained. On the one hand, she should have felt happy. Florez had given her first-hand accounts of some of the things Wayland and Carrer had paid him to do to gain leverage over the girls they were abusing. It was good, and it would definitely help her story.

On the other hand, an uneasy feeling in the pit of Sam's stomach told her that Florez couldn't be trusted. Sam got the idea that behind the whole narcissistic, empty-headed, playboy persona that Florez perpetuated, there was a cold, calculating mind at work.

Not once during the interview had Florez expressed guilt or shame for what he had done. He told his part in it with a sick sort of relish that was also removed as if he was pitching an interesting script to a director rather than admitting to various crimes.

Either he was delusional and still thought he was going to come out of all this with just a little slap on the wrist, or there was some other game at play that Sam wasn't yet seeing.

If he was delusional, that meant he didn't think what they did was so bad. Then, he was one of those men who believed all women wanted him, and those who said no were just playing games. Sam could see him thinking like that. He certainly seemed like the type.

The idea that she would have to be sitting across from him again the following day made Sam feel dirty. She packed up her stuff and headed out. It was already early in the evening. She needed dinner, a shower, and a few hours of watching some mindless TV show to calm her nerves before she went to bed.

Climbing in her car, Sam had a flashback of Florez's face as he told her about being intimate with the girls. The glitter in his eyes gave her the impression that he was perhaps even turned on while telling her about it.

Sam mentally revised her plan for the evening and decided dinner and TV could wait. What she needed most right then was a shower. And perhaps a stiff drink.

Chapter 10:

Eyes Everywhere

Sam's whole plan for a quiet evening flew out the window as she stopped in the driveway of the holiday house and saw Ryan and Kyle standing outside. Kyle was standing with his hands in his pockets, his head bent morosely. Ryan had his arms folded over his chest and looked up as he saw Sam step out of the car.

She glanced at the house. It looked fine, except for the fact that it was dark inside. She wondered, with a sinking feeling in her gut, why the men hadn't gone inside.

"Hey, guys, what's up?" She didn't get the usual warm greeting from either of them, and that didn't bode well.

Ryan turned away angrily, and Kyle raked his fingers through his hair in frustration. Then, he turned to Sam, and she saw that he wasn't angry but scared.

"Someone broke in, Sam. It doesn't look like your typical burglary. We didn't want to disturb anything in case you wanted to call the police."

Sam walked past them without saying anything else and stepped inside.

She noticed that one of the glass panes on the front door was broken. It was how the burglar had gained access to the house. Sam's shoes made a crunching noise on the pieces of broken glass as she walked further into the house.

She stood in the entryway and glanced inside the living room. The TV was still there, and nothing seemed out of place.

Sam walked through the entire house, room by room. The game room downstairs, the one she had been using as an office because of the large desk in one of the corners, seemed to be the only room that had been disturbed.

Sam's research papers had been thrown everywhere. Photos and recordings of witness accounts lay scattered across the floor. Sam stepped over to the desk where empty folders were spread out, along with her laptop, which now had a cracked screen. Sam picked it up and checked, but the laptop didn't seem to be working.

Sam gathered the scattered paperwork into a bundle, along with the scattered disks. When she turned around, she saw what had been left on the opposite wall. In big, ugly letters, someone had used red spray paint to write the single word "BITCH" all in capital letters.

Maybe she was numb from shock, but this obvious tactic to scare her didn't even make her angry. All she felt was tired. The thought of having to find a new place to sleep that night and all the nights to come did nothing to lift her spirits. She knew she could no longer stay at the holiday house. It wouldn't be safe.

As she gathered all the stuff into a duffel bag she found in the closet, she wondered where she should go. A hotel seemed most likely.

Sam was glad they hadn't taken all her stuff, but now Carrer knew what the burglar knew. Luckily, she had been using aliases for her key witnesses. If Carrer tried to track down those names, as Sam was sure he would, he would reach a dead end.

Sam went over to one of the portraits hanging on the wall. Behind it was a safe that she opened, and inside were the hard copies of the interviews with her key witnesses, as well as files where the key witnesses were mentioned by name. The burglar hadn't opened the safe, she was sure of it.

There were other things in the safe that were now important. Cash because she would no longer be able to use her credit cards, fake ID, and driver's license that she had obtained for just such an emergency.

When Sam was done, she put her bag in the living room and went outside to speak to Kyle and Ryan again. Sam already had a suspicion about what Kyle was going to tell her.

During her search through the house, she peeked inside the bedroom that Ryan and Kyle shared. Their closets were standing open and empty. Since nothing else seemed to be missing in the room besides their own personal belongings, Sam guessed that they had already packed all their stuff and were leaving.

When Sam got outside, she saw that Kyle was leaning against the car. Ryan was inside the car, behind the steering wheel. She couldn't understand why he seemed angry with her. Did he really blame her for all of this?

Kyle came over to her awkwardly, "Sam, listen... I..."

He didn't seem capable of finishing his sentence, so Sam finished it for him. "You want out?"

Kyle was biting his lip and looking at her sadly. Clearly, he felt bad for abandoning her and walking away. She decided not to make it harder for him than necessary. There was one thing she did want to ask him, though.

The ghost of a smile flitted across Kyle's face before he could compose his features. "We're finally doing it and moving to Portugal. You know, it's what we always dreamed of doing."

In the few months that Sam got to know the two men better, she understood that they had been talking about moving to Portugal for the longest time, basically since they started dating. Sam had no idea, specifically, why Portugal was the dream, but she thought it was a beautiful dream to have and that they would eventually do it in a few years when they finished saving up for it.

From the many conversations Sam had with them about it, she knew they still had a long way to go financially before the dream could become a reality. Kyle wasn't exactly earning mega bucks at his job. Ryan was a small business owner, and from what Sam could gather, some months he did well, and other months he barely broke even.

How did they get their hands on enough money all of a sudden?

As if picking the question right out of her mind, Kyle explained, "Ryan's one uncle passed away a few months ago, and he didn't think the guy would leave him anything. It turns out he did, and with the money we already had saved up, it's finally enough."

Sam saw the pleading look in Kyle's eyes and understood that he wanted to believe what Ryan was telling him and where this sudden windfall came from. She also understood that Kyle didn't quite believe it. One word from Sam and Ryan's flimsy story would make it fall apart.

"Well, I'm very happy for both of you. It's a shame you don't have time to celebrate, but I understand. It's not safe for either of you around me right now."

Watching them drive away, Sam felt an uneasy mix of loneliness, betrayal, and relief.

She knew it was Ryan who had given up the location of the holiday house where the three of them had been hiding. Carrer or someone close to him had paid Ryan enough to finance their dream.

Sam thought back to the past few months, reflecting on how things had been for the guys and how their lives had been turned upside-down by all of this. She could have ruined their relationship by exposing Ryan's betrayal, but to what end? Kyle would have resented her for it, and the damage was already done.

As Sam walked back to the house to finish packing her clothes and other belongings, she thought that at least Ryan hadn't told them about the safe where the really valuable evidence was stored. Ryan had known about it but had risked Carrer's men not finding exactly what they were looking for and taking it out on him and Kyle. That was why Ryan was so eager to leave, besides the fact that Carrer now knew where all of them were hiding out.

Back in the house, Sam finished packing quickly and got into her car. It was too late in the evening to find a new laptop, a new car, or any of the other things she would need. The best she could do was to find a cheap motel for the night, get some food and some sleep, and try to figure out her next step in the morning when her mind was a bit clearer.

As Sam drove down the street, a pair of headlights from a car coming from the opposite direction nearly blinded her. As they passed each other, Sam glanced at the driver quickly and then looked away. She suppressed the urge to put her foot down on the gas, knowing that doing so would alert the two men in the car that she was the woman they were looking for. Her quick glance had confirmed it was Carrer's men. One of them was the guy that Sam had first noticed following her when she hid in the changing room at the clothing store.

Part of Sam was yelling that she should just go and drive away as quickly as possible. Her curiosity won, and when she reached the end of the street, she drove around the block. As she went down the street again, she switched off her headlights. It was a small block of very few houses, so by the time Sam was driving up to her father's house again, the car had just parked underneath a tree, avoiding the glare of the street light.

Sam parked the car a good distance away and watched what the men in the vehicle did next.

After a few minutes of silently canvassing the street, both men got out of the car. Sam's blood froze when one of the men put on a pair of leather gloves as they walked quietly up to the house. The guy that Sam recognized was holding something, hiding it under his jacket.

It was a gun. Sam was sure of it. These two men had been sent to kill her, possibly Ryan and Kyle, too.

Sam watched one of them stick his hand through the broken glass and open the door from the inside. Then, the two men went inside the house and closed the door behind them.

Sam had seen enough. She switched on the car and drove to the end of the street again. Then, she turned in the direction of the main road.

After about an hour of driving around aimlessly, Sam realized she was in a complete daze. She stopped in front of a motel, just the sort of place she had been looking for. After checking in, giving the fake ID to the grumpy woman at the front desk, and getting her key, Sam took the duffel bag with the evidence and a small overnight bag from the car. If someone wanted to steal the rest of her stuff while she was asleep, they were welcome to do so as far as she was concerned.

Sam barely looked at the room after she closed the door. She kicked off her shoes and fell onto the bed, clothes and all, without bothering to pull back the covers. She didn't fall asleep so much as she was overtaken by it.

For the next 12 hours, Sam slept without dreaming.

Chapter 11:

Bate and Switch

Sam's heart was galloping in her chest. Her breath came in short, little gasps. Drawing it in between her cracked, dry lips, she swallowed and gulped as she ran. Her footfalls echoed loudly in the warehouse, bouncing off the stacked crates that she knew were just for show. The warehouse's interior was like a maze. She rounded a corner and then crouched down behind one of the huge plastic containers. Closing her mouth so she would be breathing through her nose, Sam tried to stay perfectly still while listening.

Then, she heard it. The sound of someone approaching.

She looked up and saw an opening between two of the plastic containers that created a little space. Sam crawled across the floor on her hands and knees and into the space. She had only just turned and pulled her feet in when the man chasing her rounded the corner and stopped. Sam could hear him breathing. He was more out of breath than she was. She heard him swear under his breath when he saw the empty passage of containers and realized that Sam was no longer there. Would he continue searching for her, or would he give up and go away? Sam didn't hold out much hope for the latter.

As she waited with bated breath to see what he would do, Sam thought back to a week earlier, when Florez had told her about the chatroom used by Carrer's inner circle to communicate with coded messages. Each of the users used aliases, so they wouldn't be able to identify each other if one of them got caught and decided to give the police the details of the chatroom as leverage. Still, Sam thought there was some way she could use the chatroom to her advantage. And she was right.

Finding herself alone after her last hideout had been broken into, Sam knew that she needed some way to throw Carrer off her trail. She needed to give him something to focus on to buy her more time.

With Florez's help, Sam had set up a user profile that would grant her access to the chatroom. It was one of his old usernames, so it wouldn't draw suspicion when Sam logged in and suddenly appeared among the men chatting there. After a few days of watching and reading the messages, looking for tone, and taking into consideration everything she knew about both Carrer and Wayland, she thought she had identified them in the chatroom.

Reading between the lines, Sam knew when they were talking about her. They gave her the moniker Lois, Sam thought, after the character Lois Lane, who was Superman's love interest and also a reporter. From the messages, Sam saw that a few of the other men were livid with Carrer for his inability to silence Sam so far.

Because she hadn't quite trusted Florez, Sam had decided to set up a sting operation where she led Carrer and the rest of them to believe that Florez had gotten wind of an exposé she was planning. She told Florez that it was just a ruse. If it worked, then she would know Florez wasn't working as a double agent, and she could trust him. If it didn't work, then Florez were indeed still feeding information behind Sam's back to Carrer and the rest of them.

Sam had reached out to Detective Michael Hall, one of the only detectives still working on Maxine Wilson's case, trying to find the missing girl. He was also the only detective who didn't believe Chloe Wilcox had run away from home. Like Sam, Michael had put two and two together. He suspected that Wayland Scott was involved in a human trafficking ring and that those two girls had been part of it. Sam gave Michael the information she had so far, and he helped her set up a sting operation where they could catch one of the guys in Carrer's inner circle.

Pretending to be Florez, Sam dropped a rumor in the chatroom that he suspected Sam had gotten wind of the warehouse where some of the girls had previously been kept. That information had unfortunately died with Pierre Travis. At the time of his death, Sam had still been trying to convince Pierre to take her there. Carrer wouldn't know if Pierre had given her the information or not. Sam, pretending to be Florez, had given the men in the chatroom the warehouse address, suggesting it would be as good a place as any to silence her forever. Sam knew that Carrer would consider the possibility that it could be a trap. On the other hand, he was desperate to find her, and dangling the possibility that she would be vulnerable and alone, chasing down a false lead in front of them, would make it very hard for Carrer and his associates to resist.

Sam had shown up at the warehouse earlier that night as planned. She had made a show of breaking in and had started taking photos of the barrels and crates in case she was being watched. That was when someone—a man wearing a mask—stepped out of the shadows and called Sam's name. She had expected the police, Michael and his team, to come and arrest the man. When that didn't happen, Sam realized the police weren't there. She was trapped in the warehouse with a masked man intent on killing her.

After distracting him, Sam started running and has been chased by the man ever since. Now, she was exhausted, and so was he. She knew this chase couldn't go on much longer. As she sat in the cramped space, considering her predicament, Sam wondered what had happened to Detective Michael Hall. He seemed like a straight arrow, genuinely concerned for the girls and, like her, desperate to uncover the truth. Had Carrer gotten to him? Threatened him or paid him off? Sam found it difficult to believe that, but his absence there now spoke volumes.

Sam jumped when the masked man started yelling her name. "Sam! Samantha King!" His voice was muffled slightly because of the ski mask he was wearing. He pulled off the mask. Sam knew he had when he spoke again, and his voice was clearer. "I was sent here to kill you, but I want to cut a deal instead!"

Sam leaned forward in the small space, curious to see the face of the man who had come to kill her. It was impossible to see clearly, and all she could make out was a pair of scuffed cowboy boots.

"Look, I'm putting down my gun!" She heard him take the clip out of his pistol, and he put both his empty gun and the clip down on the floor and kicked them forward out of reach. They slid across the floor and came to a stop right in front of Sam.

She was biting her lip, wondering what to do. He could have another gun on him, but why the ruse then? Was it just to draw her out? He didn't react when Sam reached out and grabbed the gun.

She retreated into her small space and put the clip back in the gun. Now armed, she crawled out of her hiding place and stood up to face the man, who, just moments before, she thought was trying to kill her.

As Sam looked at the scraggly-faced man standing before her, he said, “Your police friends are not coming. Carrer put pressure on Detective Hall’s boss. Detective Hall got fired today, so he’s no longer a detective.”

“What do you want from me?” Sam asked curiously. “Why are you here?”

The man looked at her with eyes that told her nothing of what he was feeling. He gave Sam the creeps. “When you publish your story, I want my name to be kept out of it. I’m not like the other guys. I didn’t take pleasure in hurting those girls. Carrer and I have known each other since college. We were good friends, but he was sort of selfish, you know? I wrote it off as coming from a rich family. My parents were barely scraping by to put me through college, and I was working two jobs to sustain that. One night, we were at a sorority party, and I ended up making out with this girl. We were both pretty wasted. When we woke up, she was sitting on one corner of the bed, holding the sheet over herself and crying, telling me I had drugged and raped her. I wanted to deny it, but when I tried to think back to what actually happened, I couldn’t remember either. Carrer showed up, saying he had heard her crying and asking if he could help. I told him I thought someone drugged both me and the girl as a prank. Carrer told me not to worry, and he'd sort it out. He took the girl home, and there were no charges pressed then or later. I heard through the grapevine that she had gone back home to whatever small town she hailed from. I didn't think of the incident again until years later. Carrer asked me for a favor, and I said no. That's when he showed me the video of me and the girl. He had recorded it on his phone. I was screwing her, and he took a close-up of her face. It was clear that she was unconscious at the time. I was so out of it, but who would believe a guy when he said that his best friend roofied him just to get dirt on him? He has been using it against me for years. I want to be done with him and the whole sorry business."

As he spoke, it dawned on Sam why he looked so familiar. "You're Mitch Greystone, the director!"

Mitch nodded but didn't say anything else. His proposition was made. It was in Sam's court now.

Mitch Greystone had been an award-winning director until a few years ago. Hollywood gossip columns had whispered about alcoholism, professional burnout, and drug abuse. Now, Sam wondered if being involved with Carrer's elicit activities hadn't led to massive depression. It certainly seemed that way listening to his story.

"How do I know I can trust you? How do I know you have anything valuable to give me?"

Mitch seemed to be thinking for a moment. "I can take you somewhere. Somewhere you'll be able to get video footage that conclusively proves what Carrer has been up to."

"Where is it?" Sam was curious, despite not trusting Mitch.

"No, Miss King. It doesn't work like that. You have to promise me that you'll keep my name out of your story and that you'll make sure the story you write will put Carrer behind bars. That's the deal. I need my life back."

Finally, Sam nodded, and Mitch followed her to her car. Walking with him alone in the dark, Sam couldn't help but feel uneasy, as this would be another perfect moment for Mitch to attack her if that was his plan all along, or even if he changed his mind. She felt a chill run down her spine.

Just before getting into her car, she stopped and held out the pistol for Mitch to take. He smiled and shook his head. "Nah, maybe you should hold on to that. It's unregistered, so don't get caught with it. I have another one."

He closed her door for her after she got in. "I'll just bring my motorcycle around, and you can follow me to the first location."

The first? Sam's curiosity was killing her. She waited silently for Mitch to return. She felt nervous and keyed up, drumming her fingers on the steering wheel.

Suddenly, a strange face appeared at her window. It almost gave Sam a heart attack, but it was just Michael.

Sam unlocked the passenger door and gestured for him to get in. As Michael was closing the passenger door behind him, he turned to Sam. "Don't know if you heard."

"That you got fired today? Yeah, I heard. Hate to break it to you, but I think someone high up in your department is in Carrer's pocket."

Michael agreed, and Sam gave him a rundown of her conversation with Mitch Greystone. Just as Sam finished telling it, they saw the headlights of Mitch's motorcycle appear. Sam turned the ignition switch, and the car roared to life.

"Well," she said. "Here we go. I just hope it's really something useful that he wants to show me."

Chapter 12:

Behind Locked Doors

Following Mitch through the dark back alleys, both Sam and Michael had time to wonder where they were going. It was clear that Mitch was leading them to a secluded area just off the edge of Capitol Hill and above Lakeview Boulevard.

Looking around, Sam realized she had never been in that area before and had no idea what to expect. They followed Mitch down a winding road where the blooming Northern Red Oaks encroached and formed natural curtains, every now and again giving glimpses of the city lights twinkling far below them in the distance.

They lost sight of Mitch when his motorcycle turned right and disappeared. Sam eased the car down a dirt road, hoping they wouldn't end up stuck with no way to get out.

At the end of the dirt road, they came to a large iron gate. Sam wondered if they would be going on foot the rest of the way, but Mitch parked his bike, jumped off, and opened the gate. He waved them through, and they proceeded to drive a little way down the road before the dense oak trees opened up to reveal a dark and looming mansion with ivy growing up its sides. All the windows were dark and curtainless, giving the place a definite abandoned feel. Sam noticed that the stone pillars holding the balcony over the front door seemed to have crumbled a bit. There were sections of stone and plaster missing, lying on the wooden porch.

Sam knew that this was where they were supposed to be and could already guess that Carrer must still be the owner of the property, though it didn't look like anyone was living there at the moment. Looking up at the dark windows, now illuminated by the headlights of her car, the whole place gave Sam the chills, and she wondered what dark secrets this house hid within its walls.

Sam and Michael stepped out of the car, and the only sound was their footfalls crunching loudly on dried leaves and loose stones that the ground was littered with. Mitch came up to them nervously and handed Sam a flashlight. He only glanced briefly at Michael and didn't ask any questions about the ex-detective's sudden appearance. This told Sam that he recognized Michael. So many questions tumbled through Sam's mind about how much Carrer and his associates really knew about her investigation, but there was no time to ask as Mitch turned around and led the way up the stone steps to the house's glass-paneled front doors.

Two lions, sleeping on their front paws, stood on either side of the large doors. It gave the whole place a gothic feel, and again, Sam felt a chill run down her spine as she thought of ghosts in abandoned mansions.

There was a tinkling sound as Mitch took a bundle of keys out of his pocket to unlock the doors. "I'm the caretaker of a few of Carrer's properties. There are two others I'll take you to after this one. This was the one most recently used, though. No one lives here. I suppose I could have told you what they were used for, and I guess both of you already have some idea. I'd rather just show you. Talking about it..." He didn't finish his sentence, so Sam had to fill in the blanks for herself.

They stepped into the house, and Mitch spoke to them over his shoulder. "There is working electricity, but I don't want to risk someone driving by and seeing the lights on, wondering why that is. Especially not someone who knows the place is supposed to look abandoned."

He saw them frowning and gave a self-conscious little laugh. "Yeah, I know I sound paranoid, but... I guess I'm just feeling guilty about betraying Carrer by bringing you here."

Sam and Michael looked around, taking in what details they could of the house illuminated by the yellow beam of the flashlight. Peeking around the arched entrance that seemed to lead into a parlor area, Sam saw a few pieces of furniture standing in a haphazard fashion. The furniture looked like expensive antiques, which made her wonder why they had been left behind when the house was not in use. Wouldn't it have been better to put them in storage instead of allowing them to rot away like that? Maybe Carrer, being as rich as he was, had a disregard for valuable things of beauty.

Mitch led them to a hallway set in the middle of the house, where a spiraling staircase led to the second floor. At first, Sam thought that Mitch was going to take the stairs. Instead, he walked into the room, bent down, and lifted the loose carpet up by one corner. It revealed a hatch in the floor. Mitch found the latch, lifted the section of the floor, and revealed a staircase going down. It was pitch black inside. Sam could only see the first few steps. She wasn't normally afraid of the dark, but the idea of sinking into that particular darkness made her feel claustrophobic.

Mitch must have seen the look of panic on Sam's face. "Don't worry, I'll go first and switch the lights on. No risk of them being spotted from the outside of the house. There are no windows down there."

Sam watched with apprehension as Mitch walked down the steps. He wasn't so much walking into the darkness as being swallowed alive by it. As he found and flicked the light switch, Sam felt a sense of relief wash over her. Whatever horrible things she and Michael would have to face down there, at least they wouldn't have to do it in the dark.

Michael elected to walk down the steps first. Then, it was Sam's turn. When she got about halfway down, she saw that the two men were waiting for her. After the darkness of the house, the lights seemed particularly bright. They came from a whole row of fluorescent lights attached to the basement's roof.

As Sam looked down the long hallway with its cement floor, she saw row upon row of prison cells with steel bars on either side. It reminded her of every prison movie she had ever seen. As far as Sam could see, every cell was empty except for a dirty blanket and pillow in a few of them, bundled into one corner of the cell. Each cell had its own wash basin and toilet. There were no mirrors. Still, the place seemed to have been kept almost surgically clean. Its many surfaces glittered in the fluorescent lights, and Sam could detect the faintest whiff of disinfectant in the air.

"Carrer essentially pays me to come and clean the place after one of his parties. The girls stay here for up to twenty-four hours. Those that survive are medically treated and then sold to an overseas buyer at a discounted price. Damaged goods."

Sam had suspected as much, but hearing Mitch so casually confirm those suspicions, she felt her stomach clench with disgust. She got out her camera and started taking pictures—anything to focus her attention on so she wouldn't slap Mitch for his part in this horror. "Tell me about these parties."

Mitch shook his head. "I can't tell you the names of the people who attend because I'm never on the guest list." Then, because he could see that Sam didn't believe him, he said, "This is not my thing, okay? The guys that Carrer invites either pay top dollar or they have something else that Carrer wants."

"You're an award-winning director, and you're telling me that Carrer just uses you as a caretaker and cleaning service?"

"Well, he needs someone to do it, and he's got me right where he wants me, doesn't he? But no, that's not all I do. I also edit the footage of the videos they make sometimes, those that Carrer also sells, distributes, or uses as leverage."

At the end of the hallway, there were a series of closed doors. Mitch opened one of them and led the way inside. Here, Sam felt again as if she had walked onto a movie set. She had seen Hollywood representations of BDSM. Not being into that lifestyle herself, Sam had still realized that the depiction of it was usually unrealistic, if not downright false. Theoretically, Sam had no problem with it if done between consenting adults. She knew there was a whole community of people living that life happily. This, however, wasn't even close to that. It was a torture chamber. There was a type of bed set in the middle of the room, covered with black rubber sheeting. Stains from some sort of dark substance were visible on its surface. Sam guessed that it was blood. She wasn't about to touch it to find out. It lay in pools and smeared on the plastic sheeting. She took pictures. The blood was still fresh enough to appear tacky and gleaming.

Pushed to one side was a table with instruments of torture, some of them still bloody, standing silently and waiting.

Sam's camera clicked as she took pictures, one after the other. She was horrified by what she was seeing but also excited. *This is it*, she thought over and over again. *I've got him*. The thought was like a mantra, giving her the strength to continue.

After taking pictures of the table with its whips and metal-studded planks of all sizes, Sam turned back to the bed. She took a pen out of her pocket and hooked one of the empty steel handcuffs that were attached to one end of a long chain. This chain was bolted to the underside of the bed. There were two handcuffs and two larger leg restraints. Sam didn't want to touch the empty cuff, but she wanted the perfect shot. She placed the empty cuff, yawning open, on the top of the bed. Looking at the image through her camera, Sam again felt that thrill of excitement. This was it—the perfect shot. This image would be at the top of her article when she published it. It told a very specific story so completely that the reader would immediately get an idea of the narrative to follow.

"Sam, I think you better come over here and take a look at this."

Sam turned around and saw Michael standing behind a tripod that held a mini camera. She had been so focused on the blood-splattered bed and the tools of torture that she hadn't noticed the camera.

Mitch was standing in one corner of the room with his hands in his pockets. Now, he spoke up. "It's the reason I brought you here first. This event was hosted two days ago. Usually, I'd just clean up and take the camera home, download the footage from it, and, after editing, give it to Carrer on a memory stick. Then, I saw who the person in the footage was. When Carrer told me about you," Mitch nodded to Michael, "and that Sam was working with you on the case, I knew I had a chance to end it all. To bring this whole thing down. To finally be free of it."

Burning with curiosity now, Sam leaned over Michael's shoulder as he pressed play on the video camera. When they saw the restrained, naked girl and knew what was coming, Sam let out a grunt of disgust. Michael pressed fast forward, so at least the video would move fast. Eventually, they would have to watch the entire thing. For now, Michael just wanted to skip forward so they could get a glimpse of the other person on the video.

The man came into view—an older, tall, and imposing figure, bare-chested—stepping over to the bed where the terrified girl lay squirming. He had one of the studded wooden planks in his hand and took obvious pleasure in watching the girl's face contort with fear as he approached. Just before raising the torture instrument in the air, and just before bringing it down on the vulnerable young girl's naked flesh, he turned and grinned at the camera.

Beside Sam, Michael let out a hiss of surprise. He turned to Sam, wide-eyed. "That's the police chief! My boss, Jeff Malcolm. That's the guy who fired me for digging into Carrer's business!"

At least now they knew why the police chief had been adamant about protecting Carrer—because he was part of Carrer's inner circle.

Sam didn't know yet what they were going to do with this evidence. She only knew that whatever they did, it was going to set the world as they knew it on fire.

Chapter 13:

Web Unraveled

Michael poured over the article while Sam sipped her coffee. They were sitting at the breakfast counter in his sunny, spacious kitchen. He had inherited the house from his parents when they passed away 10 years earlier.

He hadn't been too thrilled about seeing Sam at his front door so early in the morning, not because he didn't want to see her, but because he knew she had risked her own safety to come and see him. Bringing him the preliminary report *The Telegraph* had published had only been an excuse. She just wanted to see him.

Both of them knew that something was happening between them. They were more than friends, more like comrades fighting together in the trenches. A physical relationship would be a bad idea just then, but Sam was looking forward to exploring exactly what they could be once the human trafficking story was over.

In bold letters across the front page, the article heading proclaimed, "Sex, Torture, and Murder: The Truth Behind Colmbs Carrer's Music Empire." Underneath was the picture that spoke a thousand words: the bed covered in black rubber and blood, with one open handcuff beckoning to the darkest corners of the reader's imagination.

It was very effective, and Michael was impressed with Sam's obvious writing skills. He could see Sam was happy, relieved, and relaxed. That worried him because he knew this article would open the floodgates of public scrutiny. When that happened, Sam's feeling of triumph would collapse. Both of them still had a while to go before this whole mess would truly be over.

After leaving the house where they had made their grisly discoveries, Mitch had taken them to three more locations. At each of the properties, the house itself, clearly abandoned, was just window dressing. Underneath each of them, they discovered the cells—the private rooms used for the god-awful entertainment and sexual depravity of Carrer himself and his closest friends and business associates who shared his dark desires. None of the other locations proved to be such a treasure chest for discovering evidence—for him and Sam—but since all of them were still registered under either Carrer's name or the name of his company, it was important to gather all the evidence from them to investigate and take pictures.

That was one of the longest nights of Michael's life, let alone his career. Afterward, they parted ways with Mitch and assured him they'd be in touch. Then, Michael followed Sam to her hotel room, where she made copies of the video. She gave one copy to Michael. Sam assured him that she'd be putting two of the other copies away for safekeeping in case something happened to both of them. Neither of them wanted the story to die with them if Carrer succeeded in killing them. It was too important. Sam wanted to make sure that Carrer didn't win. The almost disastrous sting operation that could very easily have resulted in Sam being killed hadn't been lost on her. She knew that when Carrer got wind of her knowing about the basement rooms, he would be even more desperate to silence her.

Now, it was too late. The story had gone out that morning. Last night, Michael had the distinct pleasure of being present when Internal Affairs went to arrest Jeff Malcolm, the police chief. He had told Sam afterward, with grim satisfaction, how Malcolm had almost fainted when confronted with the video as evidence of his arrest. Michael had been reinstated as a detective with immediate effect after he had presented all the evidence to Internal Affairs. The four locations of the torture chambers were even then being overturned by forensic teams gathering DNA samples.

Sam wondered how many of the DNA samples would be connected in the end with the missing girls. Only time would tell, and it wasn't going to happen overnight. In the end, Carrer might even be able to cut a deal with the prosecution if he gave up the location of where the bodies of the victims were buried—if that was at all a possibility. That thought didn't sit comfortably with Sam. She wanted Carrer to be sentenced to the maximum number of years that his crimes warranted. Anything less would be a slap in the face for the victims and their families. Unfortunately, that wasn't up to Sam or Michael and was, in fact, completely out of their hands.

Carrer would do his best to discredit Sam, but she was prepared for that and ready to face what was coming. She said as much to Michael when he expressed his concern regarding the backlash she was bound to face.

They talked for a few minutes longer, and then Sam told him she had to go. She was needed at the offices of *The Seattle Telegraph* because, apparently, there were already a number of people waiting to speak to her—girls who had stories to tell about the abuse they had faced at the hands of Carrer and Wayland. The publication of the first story gave the witnesses new hope.

"That's great! I'm glad they're finally coming forward. Maybe they'll get some sense of peace just telling their story to another person willing to hear them out."

"Maybe," Sam smiled secretly. Considering what the girls and young women had been through, she thought that only seeing the perpetrators behind bars for their crimes would do that.

Michael waited with Sam outside on his porch for the Uber. Sam got in the back seat and waved a little goodbye. Michael got a glimpse of the driver's dark eyes in the rearview mirror, watching Sam. He frowned and felt an uneasy flutter in the pit of his stomach.

Before he could analyze what he was feeling and act accordingly, the car was already speeding away. Michael watched the Uber tear down the street. Either Sam had just gotten the Uber driver from hell, or that wasn't her ride. His worst fears were realized when another car stopped in the street a second or two later, and the driver glanced up and down the street in confusion.

The driver rolled down his window and asked, "Sorry, I'm supposed to pick someone up from this address."

Michael waved the guy away. He was already running back into the house for his car keys and service weapon. Everything was lying on a shelf in the living room. He grabbed his badge as well because it was right there. As he ran outside to his car, he recalled every detail he could about the car that had picked Sam up.

Driving down the same road, Michael felt like he was in a life-and-death race against time. He was sure that the kidnapper must be connected to Carrer. What were they planning? Was the driver taking Sam so Carrer could confront her, or would he simply kill Sam and dump her body? Michael had no idea, but given what he knew about Carrer, he would bet on the former. Carrer was a very arrogant individual, thinking he was above the law because of his wealth. Sam had proven to be a formidable adversary. Michael thought that Carrer would want to face her and kill her himself, proving that he still held the most power.

Michael was surprised when, about 10 minutes later, he got to the scene of a car crash. He recognized the car that Sam had disappeared in only a few minutes before. Now, the car was standing haphazardly, smoking from a busted radiator leaking fluid. The nose of the car was smashed up against a tree at the side of the road. The driver's door was standing open.

Michael stopped his own car and rushed to the passenger side. Sam was inside, unconscious. Panicking now, Michael opened the door and caught Sam before she could fall out of the car. He felt for a pulse and found one. Her heartbeat was strong, and the rhythm was regular. He checked her for a gunshot wound or knife wound but couldn't find any source of bleeding or broken bones. It seemed that she had just passed out. He laid her down on the back seat of the car and went to check the driver's side, though he had already seen that the driver must have fled. Michael found a single shoelace on the ground on the driver's side.

Staring at it in confusion, he phoned in the accident and gave a description of the driver. He wasn't holding out much hope for the guy's arrest. If he was a hired killer, then he would know how to disappear fast.

When the ambulance came, they found the reason why Sam was unconscious. There was a serious electrical burn wound on her wrist. It was consistent with being shocked with a taser set at a high voltage. "She's lucky her heart didn't stop," the EMT told Michael as he rode with Sam in the back of the ambulance.

Sam woke up a few minutes later. "When I realized I was being kidnapped, I unlaced one of my shoes. I strangled him with the shoelace to make him crash the car. I figured it was better to die in a car crash than whatever Carrer had planned for me."

They took Sam to the hospital, where they treated her wound. Michael went down to a vending machine to get them some coffee. When he came back, Sam was having a heated argument with the doctor.

She looked over at Michael for support, but the doctor also turned to Michael, interrupting her before she could appeal her case.

"Your friend is very stubborn. We should be keeping her overnight for observation, but she's refusing to be admitted!"

This wasn't surprising. Michael had expected some resistance from Sam about staying the night. "Listen to the doctor. Let them take care of you. You can follow up with the witnesses tomorrow. They'll still be there, willing to talk to you then."

Sam shook her head adamantly. "If Carrer can get to me, then eliminating as many of the witnesses as possible shouldn't be a problem."

Michael wanted to put Sam at ease because part of him wanted her taken care of. He had feelings for her. His concern for her safety when he thought she was gone had proven that to him beyond a shadow of a doubt.

Another part of him, the voice of practicality and reason, argued that Sam's life wasn't more important than the victims' lives. It wasn't more important than the lives of so many other girls sold into slavery, who may still be somewhere praying for rescue to come even as they were being assaulted and abused. What hope did they have but Sam, willing to risk everything for them to finally be freed and reunited with their loved ones? Was Maxine Wilson among those still waiting?

He was just about to open his mouth to tell the doctor to patch Sam up and let her go, that they had somewhere else they needed to be, when Sam's cell phone rang.

As she answered it, the doctor, completely out of patience now, threw up his hands in disgust and left the room in an angry huff.

The call only took a few moments. When it was over, Sam looked at Michael, her eyes rounding with worry. "That was a trusted source of mine, someone else from Carrer's inner circle. He just called to inform me that Wayland Scott committed suicide early this morning. Apparently, the note he left in his own blood on the tiles of the bathroom wall was an admission of guilt that would stand up in any courtroom. My source also informed me that Wayland's death seemed to have been the last straw for Carrer. He's planning to leave the country. He's going on the run."

Chapter 14:

Race Against Time

"So, where should we go first?" Michael asked as they got in his car.

"You can just drop me off at the office. I think Tony would have gotten the addresses of the witnesses and sent them home to wait for my phone call. I hope they're okay."

"You're going to be running after witnesses to get their statements? Why don't I just drive you?"

Sam shook her head. She didn't want Michael to risk his life; that was really her job. It was her story. She didn't mind risking her own neck, but she would never forgive herself if something were to happen to him.

Michael saw some of this in her eyes. He took her hand and glanced back at the road as they drove out of the parking lot and mingled with the rest of the afternoon traffic.

"Look, I'm already involved. Why don't we just skip ahead to the part where you admit we make a great team and let me help you? Besides, after what almost happened to you, I don't want you to die before I get to take you out. Considering how dangerously you live, I think we should make this our first date."

Sam blushed slightly, but she was grinning. “I don’t think this can really count as a date, though.”

Michael glanced at her and winked. “It will if we stop for lunch, and I’m buying.”

He looked up in the rearview mirror and frowned. Sam leaned over and looked in the car’s side mirror to try and see what he was looking at.

“I think we’re being followed,” Michael said grimly. “See the dark blue car? It’s been following us from the hospital. I’m going to make a few random turns to see if this is really the case.”

A few minutes later, they had confirmation that the blue car was indeed following them. “I’m going to ask Tony to meet us with the list of witnesses. If you can get us someplace where they can’t observe us, then we can wait there for Tony. We’ll have to ditch your car, though.”

“Does *The Seattle Telegraph* building have a back entrance? Security?”

Sam nodded. “Yeah. Good security since they’ve had a few bomb threats because of this story, actually. Now, no one can enter if they don’t have a security pass. The building’s back door opens into an alley that they share with a Chinese restaurant.”

“Okay, then I’ll just drive there, and you can get the info. What does it matter if these guys see us going in? They won't be able to follow, so they'll have to wait for us to come back out. We can worry about getting another car once we have the list of names."

They parked in front of *The Telegraph* building a few minutes later. Sam resisted the urge to look behind them to see if the guys in the blue car were watching them. Michael's escape plan could only work if the guys didn't know that it had been made.

At the reception desk, one of the security guards looked at Michael suspiciously until he pulled out his badge. "I'm Miss King's protection detail. She's been facing some threats."

The security guy nodded and looked at Sam. "Good job on exposing those scumbags, Miss King. I hope they all go to jail for a very long time."

Sam, knowing she had released only a preliminary report and there was still a whole bag of scandals waiting to be revealed that would shock the public even more, just thanked the guard and led Michael to the elevators.

As soon as they stepped into Tony's office, he jumped up from behind his desk. "My God, Sam! I heard you got into an accident! When you didn't come in, I had Smith go looking for you. She found the car of your Uber driver, and we've been calling hospitals all morning!"

Sam introduced Michael to her boss and briefly explained what had really happened and what they were after. When Tony finished printing the witness list, Michael explained what they would need.

Tony went to his office door, leaned his head out, and shouted that if somebody saw the Chase kid, they should send him to his office. A few seconds after Tony had taken a seat behind his desk again, a pale, bespectacled, and nervous-looking guy, who couldn't be more than 22, stepped into Tony's office. Although she had never seen Oliver Chase before, Sam didn't need any clarification as to who he was. Sam knew a college intern studying journalism and working at the paper for the summer when she saw one. There had been a few of them passing through in the years she worked for *The Telegraph*. All of them were equally petrified by Tony's gruff persona.

"I want you to go get me some Chinese at the place next door. Park in the alley next to the restaurant, not out in the street, you hear? My wife has a lunch date with a few friends there today. She has me on a diet for my cholesterol. If she gets so much whiff that I'm getting food there, I'll get into trouble. Then, I'll come back here tomorrow and take it out on you." Tony gave the kid some money, and Sam could see his hand was visibly shaking.

A few minutes after Oliver Chase was gone, Sam and Michael took the stairs down to the bottom floor and exited the building using that door. It could only be opened from the inside. They saw Tony's car, a cherry red Camaro, glittering quietly in the sun. Sam took the spare key for the car that Tony had given her out of her pocket. "I don't mind telling you, I've always wanted to drive Tony's car."

As they left the alley with the Camaro's tinted windows rolled up, they drove past Chase, carrying bags of Chinese food. Chase didn't see them; he was too intent on getting the bags of food, easily enough for three people, back to the boss. Michael felt a momentary pang of guilt, imagining the poor kid seeing the car was missing and having a panic attack at the thought of explaining to the big boss how his expensive sports car had been stolen while he was inside the restaurant buying lunch.

They didn't have time to worry about the kid, though. They only had a few hours to track down all the witnesses and get their statements to strengthen the prosecution's case against Carrer. With a little luck, they could prove that Carrer was a flight risk and shouldn't be granted bail once he was arrested.

The first person on the list, Maureen Wagner, was an exotic dancer and lived in a seedy little apartment above the club where she worked.

After knocking on her door, Sam tried calling her, and both Sam and Michael heard her phone ringing inside the apartment. Michael went and fetched the super of the building to unlock the door for them. It took some convincing, including phoning again and letting the guy hear it ring inside the apartment. He was still skeptical, though, and only agreed to open the door when Michael showed his badge.

They found Maureen lying dead in a pool of her own blood. It looked like her wrists had been slit, but Sam wondered if it wasn't Carrer's men who were already on the trail of the witnesses, trying to silence all of them before Sam got their statements. Michael phoned it into his station and explained to one of the other detectives why they couldn't stay.

Back in the car, Sam looked at the second name on the list. Martina Perez had given her address as 9050 Steward Park Avenue South, Slip 5-67, *Lullaby Dream.*

Michael checked the GPS. The address was for Parkshore Marina. "You mean she lives on a *boat*?" he asked incredulously.

Sam smiled. "Her boyfriend owns it, actually. She got kicked out of her apartment since the boyfriend's wife got Martina fired from her job after she found out about the affair. He had the boat before they got married, but prenup says the wife can't touch it. So, I guess he felt obligated to put his girlfriend up somewhere while he took care of the nasty divorce."

When they got to the marina, Sam marveled at the way Maureen lived versus the way Martina lived, as well as the similarities between most of the women who had been aspiring teenage singers or models before Carrer got to them. Martina's getting involved with a married man and her lifestyle choices could be indicative of her traumatic past. Not all women who were abused went on to lead less-than-ideal lives. Not all women who were abused slept with married men. Obviously, not all women who slept with married men were abused as children or teenagers. But there was a definite correlation between past trauma—especially if the victims never got help afterward, such as therapy or support from a family they could talk to—and risky behavior that ultimately led them to alienate themselves from potentially beneficial relationships.

When Michael and Sam found *Lullaby's Dream*, Sam called Martina to let her know they were there. "Oh, just go onto the boat and make yourselves comfortable. There are cold cokes in the fridge and stuff to eat. I promise I'm like 5 minutes away."

"That's weird," Sam said to Michael as they stepped onto the boat. "She said we should wait here, and she'll only be here in five minutes."

Michael, always interested in boats, was looking inside the ship's helm at the modern steering equipment. He was only listening to Sam with half an ear.

Sam opened the door to the berth area, which led to a fully equipped little kitchen, a bathroom, and a bedroom. Just as Sam put one foot forward to take a step downstairs, she felt resistance as a trip wire snagged against her leg. "Oh, shit!" she called out and stared at Michael wide-eyed. They both heard the *beep! beep!* sound and knew they only had a few seconds before something would explode.

Michael grabbed Sam's hand, and they jumped overboard together into the ocean. While they were still in the air, the bomb, set up in a closet on the ship, exploded with an ear-deafening sound. Warm air pushed them away even further, and for a few seconds, they felt as if a giant hand was carrying them along.

They landed in the water with an enormous splash, and Michael was torn away from Sam. She resisted the urge to gasp from the shock of the suddenly cold water. She knew if she did, she'd inhale water and drown. The water enveloped her, and she looked up from its murky depths and saw a sheet of fire raging just above her head.

Sam kicked and swam until she was completely clear of the burning boat. Along the way, she found Michael, who seemed to be unconscious. She dragged him by his arm and swam with him away from the wreckage that she feared would eventually attract the wrong people. As soon as they hit the surface, and Michael could breathe fresh air, he spluttered and was conscious again.

They made their way to the docks and got out. They kept shivering and dripping water all the way to the car.

"Dry clothes first before we go anywhere else," Sam said. "Tony's gonna kill me for dripping water all over his seats!"

Michael wanted to laugh at the irony of Sam being scared of Tony while, at the same time, she seemed unfazed about the fact that they had almost died, but he was still shaken. "Do you think Martina Perez was ever really one of Carrer's victims? Or did he send her to you?"

Sam thought about it. "No, I think this morning Martina was completely willing to tell me her whole story. Then, somehow, Carrer got to her and decided to use her to lead me into a trap."

Michael watched Sam as she took the list out of a file on her lap and read the names again. "Nine more names," Sam said. "How in the world are we going to find them all before Carrer gets to them? How are we supposed to know which ones we can trust?"

Michael shook his head and started the car. “I don’t know, Sam. We’ll just have to do the best we can.”

Chapter 15:

Deceptive Calm

"All set, Miss King? We'll touch up your makeup just before the camera rolls."

Sam glanced at the stylist in the mirror and smiled. "Thank you." Looking at her own reflection, she saw that her makeup was perfect, her hair done up in a sophisticated bun. She looked more elegant than she ever could have managed on her own.

Thank goodness Janice Lockland had sent her personal stylist to make all of them pretty for the camera before the interview.

"Can she at least have some of this champagne?" Tony asked and handed Sam a flute of the expensive bubbly, another courtesy from NBC Washington, one of the top-rated news channels and the one with whom Tony had struck a deal for the interview.

Janice Lockland, the investigative reporter who would be interviewing Sam and Tony for the public reveal story in less than 45 minutes, had pulled out all the stops, booking this expensive room at the Waldorf Astoria hotel. Looking at the black granite countertops, set off perfectly against the royal blue and pristine white decor, Sam could only imagine what the sitting room looked like, where a camera crew was already setting up all the fancy equipment.

Sam took the offered champagne and had a sip. Then, she stood up and followed Tony to the dining room where Michael was waiting. He also had a glass of champagne, and Sam saw with a grin how he was eyeing the service trolley that had been sent up a while ago. Sam's fluttering stomach made it impossible to think of food at the moment.

She was glad Michael was there. It was, after all, only with his help that Samantha had managed to secure the last few testimonies of the 11 victims who had wanted to come forward. They had even managed to identify the shipping yard where Carrer kept the storage containers with the girls before they were shipped to international buyers. Sam's most valuable source inside Carrer's organization, Emilio Florez, had come through and handed her this information. Log books revealed Carrer's and Louise Sutton's connection to the shipping yard, but that wasn't all. More names had been revealed, connected to the whole operation.

Sam had shared everything with the police except the names of two of these people. She was considering revealing them in the interview. The only people who currently knew of these two individuals' involvement, aside from Sam herself, were Tony and Michael. The two men whose names she had, as well as actual security footage of them meeting with Carrer in the shipping yard, were State Senator Andrew Torres and Supreme Court Judge Nicolai Salomon.

Sam was sure that if the police dug into the personal computer files of these two men, they would both be connected to the chat site where Florez, Wayland, and Carrer had communicated.

Having connected a police chief to the allegations of human trafficking had been bad enough. Now, Sam had a choice to make. She could quietly hand the police the information about Salomon and Torres and hope they would really investigate it and not squash it because of the public outrage it would cause, or she could reveal these names in a very public interview and force the hand of the police.

Michael, knowing what the stakes were, had voiced his concern for Sam herself if she set fire to the world, as she was planning to with this interview. He didn't offer advice, though, because he knew why Sam needed to go public with it. There was no telling where the loyalties lay among those at the top of the food chain, and knowing who they could trust was nearly impossible.

In the end, both Tony and Michael assured Sam that they would stand with her, regardless of what she decided to do.

That meant the world to Sam. She and Michael had turned a corner in their relationship. Following the hectic chase to find the last few witnesses, they had been flying high on adrenaline and had inevitably ended up in bed together. It could have ended there with one amazing night, but neither of them had wanted it to, and they had been dating for the past few weeks. Now, Michael was very important to her, and she felt grateful that he had come into her life despite such strange and dark circumstances.

The three of them finished their champagne and poured some more. Sam realized she was feeling uncharacteristically giddy. At least her stomach wasn't all aflutter anymore, so she had a few crackers and a bite of some sweet cheese that she didn't recognize.

The stylist appeared in the doorway and smiled at the three of them laughing together. "Thirty minutes till showtime. We can reapply your lipstick in a few minutes, Miss King."

Samantha jumped up and put her champagne down. "I better go brush my teeth. Excuse me."

She picked up the little toiletry bag that she brought along. Just then, her cell phone chimed loudly in her pocket. As she dug it out to read the message, something fell out of her pocket and skidded across the floor.

Michael picked it up and looked at it. “What’s this? Some weird sort of lipstick?”

Sam laughed. “No, you dolt. It’s a camera. You can hide it, and it records everything and can even broadcast it to your phone. Here, let me show you.”

Sam turned it on and took Michael’s phone. She showed Michael the app he had to download to connect to the camera. “See? Now I place it here.” Michael was treated to a quick view of Sam’s cleavage before she turned the camera around and placed it in her top so it peeked out. Now, he saw his own face being recorded on the phone.

Behind Sam, Tony laughed at the look on Michael’s face. “She used it to get footage of Carrer in the nightclub. It was a gift from Kyle Brenner, her assistant.”

“It was actually a gift from his boyfriend.” Sam took the camera, switched it off, and put it back in her pocket. She had worn the same jacket on the night when she had gone undercover to the nightclub. It seemed like ages ago. She felt a pang of regret, thinking of Kyle and wondering what they would think of the interview once they saw it. Sam was sure that even in Argentina, Kyle would be keeping tabs on the story to see how it progressed. She wondered if he ever felt regret that he was no longer a part of it.

Sam excused herself again and made her way to the bathroom. Her phone chimed again, and she looked at the message. It was from Florez, asking her to call him urgently. Frowning, wondering why he was contacting her now, Sam called his number.

"Hey, Emilio. I'm kind of tied up at the moment. Can I call you later?" She hadn't told him about the interview with Janice Lockland. Part of her still didn't quite trust him, especially not with the explosive information she had now. The interview wouldn't be going out live. Instead, it would be recorded, edited, and finally shown a week or two later.

"Sam? Oh, thank God I got hold of you. I need to see you as soon as possible. Can you come here to my place?"

Emilio sounded panicked. Sam did a quick calculation in her mind. Even if she left now, it would take her at least 20 minutes to reach him.

"I'm twenty minutes away, and I really can't leave right now. What's going on? Are you in danger?"

Florez assured Sam that he wasn't in any immediate danger. He said he had some important information on Carrer and insisted he tell her face-to-face.

"Why can't you just tell me over the phone?" Sam asked, but the signal seemed to be wobbly.

She realized that Emilio was driving while talking to her. She frowned. If that was the case, why did he want to meet her at his apartment?

"I can come to you. Where are you?"

Sam bit her lip. Maybe Florez knew where Carrer was hiding. Maybe Carrer had another girl somewhere, and Florez knew where he was keeping her. All the horrible possibilities were tumbling through Sam's mind, and she knew she wouldn't be able to concentrate on the interview until she heard what Florez had to say.

She told Florez where she was but didn't mention her reason for being there.

"Okay, I'm almost there. I have a room at that hotel. You can meet me in my room, and I'll give you the information. It won't take more than a few minutes." Again, Sam felt an uneasy feeling of doubt in her stomach. It seemed like too much of a coincidence that Florez just happened to be in the same area just before she was supposed to have the interview.

On the other hand, could she really say no to the information he could have? If it was as important as he said it was, then she couldn't afford to pass up the opportunity to get it. Besides, Florez said it would only take five minutes. She could get the information from him and be back in time for the interview.

Sam glanced at the bathroom door. She could faintly hear Michael and Tony speaking in the other room. The suite, which was really more like an apartment building, was filled with people who wouldn't let her leave if they knew where she was planning to go.

Sam took her lipstick in hand and quickly scribbled a message on the mirror. If she wasn't back by the time they realized she was gone, at least they would have an inkling of where she went. She was sure, with the information she had, that Janice Lockland would be willing to postpone the interview by a few minutes to give her a chance to return.

Sam opened the bathroom door quietly to see if anyone was just outside the door, but the hallway leading to the rest of the rooms and the front door were clear. She slipped out quickly. She hurried down the hallway, passing the closed door of the room where the camera crew was still setting up and getting things ready. She heard a woman's voice ordering people about and thought it was probably Janice, who must have arrived only a short while ago.

Opening the front door softly, Sam slipped out and made her way to the elevator. She pressed the button for the ninth floor.

When she came to the room Emilio had given her, she heard the sound of the television from inside. Again, Sam frowned as she realized that those were the sounds she had heard over the phone, making her think Florez was in traffic. Had Florez been in this room during their whole conversation? Part of her was screaming to just turn around and leave. But she was already there.

She stuck out her hand and knocked on the door. The television was silenced. The door opened, and Sam could see Emilio peeking out from behind the door.

"Come in, come in! Before someone sees you!"

Sam stepped inside and turned to Emilio as he closed the door. "Okay, what did you want to tell me? I have somewhere I need to be."

Emilio nodded. Sam was interested to see that he was sweating profusely—obviously nervous. It made Sam think that he really had something important to show her. He pointed to the sitting room door. "The folder on the coffee table is in there; see for yourself."

Burning with curiosity, Sam went through the doorway to the coffee table, where a blue folder was lying. Vaguely, she was aware of Emilio following behind.

"I guessed that you'd want to add this information to your interview with Janice Lockland."

Sam's hand hesitated on the folder. She was about to turn around to ask Emilio who had told him about the interview when she felt a prick in her neck. She gasped and faced Emilio, her hand now clamped to the small wound.

Florez stepped away from Sam, out of her reach. He was still holding the hypodermic needle in his hand.

"What the hell did you just inject me with?" Sam was asking, but her words were already coming out garbled. It felt like she had a ball of cotton in her mouth. She felt herself faltering and swaying. She tried to grab a nearby couch for support, but everything was swimming in front of her eyes.

As she hit the carpet, the world swam away from her, and she heard Emilio say, "Carrer told me it's fast acting. It's what he uses to silence the girls when they transport them. We're going to meet Carrer. He's waiting for you."

Chapter 16:

The Betrayer's Mask

It took a while for Sam to realize that she was awake and that her eyes were open because she was enveloped in an impenetrable darkness. She tried moving her hands and realized they were tied together. When she tried to pull her hands free from each other, her bindings bit into the flesh of her wrists. She realized that her kidnapper had used zip ties on both her hands and feet.

She tried screaming against the gag in her mouth, but the sound that came out was nothing but a pathetic mewling. For a few moments, that made her panic. She struggled and strained, tried to scream, but she could only move a few inches. The dark space she was trapped in was so small and cramped that it was like being buried alive.

Sam forced herself to relax, to think. She was lying on her side with her legs pulled up to her chin. When she tried to uncurl them, they hit against a hard surface, but whatever she was in gave a bit and bent as Sam pushed against it. The same thing happened when she tried to straighten her arms.

Now that she wasn't gripped in mindless panic anymore, she had the sensation that she was moving. Faintly, she could hear the mechanical purr of an engine and realized she was in the trunk of a car.

"What's the last thing I remember?" Sam said, and the sound of her own voice calmed her, though the words came out as an unintelligible series of huffs. She was still alive; that was the most important thing. It meant there was still hope of getting out of this.

A face swam into her memory—the handsome, worried face of Emilio Florez standing over her. Sam remembered Emilio saying he was taking her to Carrer. Just before that, the prick in her neck... Florez had drugged her, had waited until she was unconscious, and had loaded her into the trunk of his car.

Wait a minute! How would he have gotten me out of the building? I don't care how expensive the room he has at the hotel or how impressive he is as a person; they wouldn't have just let him walk out of there with an unconscious woman. Then, she realized how Florez must have done it. He had bundled her into an enormous suitcase, had loaded her on a trolley, and had gotten a bellboy or two to help him get his *luggage* downstairs and into his car. Sam giggled darkly at the thought that she was stuck inside some designer suitcase and that Florez had probably tipped the bellboys handsomely for their help in unknowingly kidnapping her.

She tried feeling along the zipper of the suitcase. Maybe there was an opening where the zipper closed? Sam found it and pushed her finger through, but the zip only moved apart a little bit, and then her finger felt there was a lock dangling from the zipper on the outside.

Sam's shoulders sagged as she realized that she wasn't going to be escaping from her confines or the trunk of the car. The best she could hope for was that some means of escape would present itself when they reached their next destination, and Florez let her out of the suitcase. Until then, she may as well relax and gather her strength.

In the darkness of the suitcase, time meant nothing. It might have been hours they traveled or days for all Sam could make out of time's passage. It gave her too much time to consider her situation and to imagine what horrible things Carrer would have in store for her once she was delivered to him.

When they eventually stopped, and Sam heard the faint sound of a car door opening and closing, she braced herself. Then, she heard the muffled sound of voices getting closer. The trunk of the car was opened, and the suitcase containing her was lifted out and placed on the ground.

When someone spoke in the world outside, it was much clearer, and Sam recognized Florez's voice. He was speaking nervously to someone, "I didn't know exactly how much to give her. I feared killing her, and I knew how badly you wanted to speak to her."

"What do you want, Emilio? A pat on the head? A gold star?" A chill ran down Sam's back as she recognized the slow, almost lazy sound of Carrer's voice. "Fine. You did well, old boy. Now, open the damn suitcase so I can see my prize."

Sam tensed, waiting... There was the jangling sound of keys and the sound of the zipper being pulled down. The sudden light blinded Sam for a moment, and then she snaked her hands out of the hole the zipper revealed. In her still-bound hands, she grabbed whatever she could find, and it just happened to be Florez's vulnerable, unsuspecting face. With her long, slender fingers, Sam pinched as hard as she could, digging her nails into his cheek and nose.

Florez yelled out and moved back, dragging Sam with him out of the suitcase. Carrer watched this development with his mouth hanging open in surprise, and then he started laughing as Florez managed to push Sam off him. Her fingernails left bleeding gashes in his cheek and over the bridge of his nose.

Florez scrambled away from her and got up off the ground. He was red in the face, clearly embarrassed and angry by Carrer's laughter. Sam glared at Florez, putting all her anger and hate into the look she gave him. Florez stepped up, pulled his foot back, and kicked her squarely in the stomach. The tip of his designer cowboy boot dug into Sam's stomach and pushed the wind out of her, making her gag violently.

Carrer grabbed Florez by the shoulder. "Come now, no damaging our guest like that. She's mine now. I promise you, before the day is out, little Miss Reporter will get what's coming to her. See if she doesn't."

He nodded to the two brutes standing on either side of him. "Bring her inside." Then, he turned around and led Florez away.

Sam leaned away from the two men, who were hired muscle dressed in black suits, but they took her by the arms and lifted her out of the suitcase, forcing her to stand.

Sam looked ahead and had a view of a mansion looming over them. They were in the driveway, the gravel crunching underneath Carrer and Florez's feet as they walked up to a marble staircase.

Then, the bigger one of the men bent in front of Sam and picked her up over his shoulder. She was carried unceremoniously to the house. She looked across the driveway and saw the mansion sitting in the middle of a dense forest of trees. Of course, Carrer would be hiding out in a place that would be difficult to find.

Sam remembered why she had been at the hotel in the first place. If she suddenly went missing, Michael and Tony would realize something had happened to her. She remembered her message scribbled in lipstick on the bathroom mirror. Just the room number where she was going, but it would be traced to Florez. Would they be able to find her after that? Would they be able to find her in time?

Following the release of her preliminary report, Carrer should have been arrested, but the police were unable to find him. That meant he was either moving around too much for them to pinpoint his exact location, or he had found a place where he could hide out until he was able to leave the country.

As she was carried up the steps and through the large doorway, Sam wondered why Carrer hadn't left the country already. Then, a cold feeling crept over her as she realized it was because he still had some unfinished business to take care of. She was his unfinished business. Getting her here, talking to her, and then killing her were important enough that he risked his window of escape. He was going to kill her, and her death wouldn't be quick or easy.

She was dumped on a chair in some sort of parlor area inside the large house. She glanced briefly at the enormous windows, where the curtains fluttered playfully in a slight breeze. It was spacious and airy in the beautifully decorated room. Sam felt a wave of unreality wash over her. She had never considered her own mortality before. If she had, she never would have thought that death would find her in a place like this.

Now, she watched Carrer. He was leaning casually against a grand piano, his fingers drumming on the closed, gleaming black lid. They were staring at each other; neither he nor Sam were willing to be the first to break eye contact. For Sam, it was like being locked in a staring contest with some sort of wild animal. Breaking eye contact may be a sign of weakness, provoking an attack.

Eventually, this silent war of wills was interrupted by Florez gently clearing his throat. “If it’s all the same to you, I would prefer to take my payment and leave.”

Carrer slowly turned his cold gaze away from Sam. His expression didn’t change as he now stared at Florez.

Emilio, clearly afraid, rubbed and brushed through his hair awkwardly. “Look, I did what we agreed on. I delivered the reporter right to you. I got her out of there before she could give the damn interview. My part is done. I’d rather not stick around for this.”

Carrer’s face split into a beautiful grin. “Why, sure. Of course... how silly of me.”

He walked over to a dark wooden cabinet standing in one corner of the room. He glanced over his shoulder as he opened the drawer. "In the end, Florez over here sold you out for $2 million, Miss King. Oh, and a new passport, identity, everything to start a new life."

Carrer opened a drawer and pulled something out. Just like Florez, she was expecting it to be an envelope with money and documents. Instead, she saw at the last moment that it was a gun and cringed. Carrer brought the gun around so quickly that no one had time to react. He fired twice, and the reports were so loud they made Sam's ears ring.

She watched in utter shock as Florez grabbed at his chest. A crimson blossom of blood was already unfolding there. Florez grabbed at the wound and looked down at his bloodied hand. Looking up at Carrer, who was still holding the gun, he opened and closed his mouth a few times, but no sound escaped from his lips. Before he could utter a word, his knees buckled out from under him, and he fell to the ground.

Walking casually, his movements fluid like those of a large cat, Carrer sauntered over to Florez, placed the gun against his temple, and pulled the trigger once more. Sam shut her eyes, but not before she saw the top of Florez's head explode in a sheet of blood, spraying brain matter across the floor.

She opened her eyes when she heard Carrer move. He walked over to the couch across from where Sam was sitting. Taking a seat, Carrer folded one leg over the other. Behind him, his two henchmen carried Florez's body out of the room and out of sight.

Sam was left alone with Carrer. Now, the gun was pointed directly at her.

Chapter 17:

Curtains Fall

"I want us to talk and for you to be as comfortable as possible while we do. So, if I remove your bindings, will you be a tiresome pest, Miss King?"

Sam slowly shook her head.

Carrer put the gun on the coffee table between them and took a small pocketknife out of the back pocket of his jeans. He bent down in front of Sam to cut the cable ties binding her feet together. While he did, Sam eyed the gun, wondering if she could kick Carrer in the face and grab it before his goons returned.

"Don't even think about it," Carrer said. He probably read what she was thinking on her face. "If you move, I'll stick this little knife straight into your thigh. If I hit your femoral artery, you'll bleed out in a couple of minutes."

Next, he uncut the bindings holding her hands together. When she could finally move them again, she took the gag out of her mouth and rubbed her wrists. Carrer had made his way back to the couch. He switched the safety on and put the gun in his coat pocket.

That reminded Sam of something. She still had the camera in her jacket pocket. By now,

Michael and the others were bound to have noticed her disappearance, would have gotten her message, and would have found Florez's room empty. They wouldn't have any idea where to go from there. Would Michael even remember the little camera she had shown him? The interaction had been so quick, but it was the only shot she had.

She reached into her pocket. Immediately, Carrer frowned at her and touched the gun in his own pocket. "Relax," Sam said, and she took the camera out. Michael thought it looked like lipstick when he first saw it. Maybe Carrer would, too. "It's only lip balm." She pretended to turn it and apply it to her lips while Carrer watched. Then, she did the same twisty motion and put the camera back in her pocket. Her finger flicked the little "On" button on the side before she turned to Carrer again. "Actually, my whole mouth is rather dry. Can I please have something to drink?"

Carrer nodded and walked over to a tray standing on an end table where alcohol in different colors was kept in crystal decanters. He poured them each a whiskey with soda and walked back, handing Sam hers.

"What is this place anyway?" Sam asked, looking around. "I guess this is where you've been hiding from the police since I released my report."

"I haven't been hiding!" Carrer barked at her. "I could have left at any time. I have the means to live somewhere else, to start with a new face and a new life before the police will even set foot here."

Sam nodded. "I wasn't being critical. Obviously, you had some unfinished business to take care of."

Carrer grinned. "Obviously." Then, he shrugged. "Fine, I don't see the harm in telling you where you'll be conducting the very last and most important interview of your life. This house belonged to my maternal grandparents."

"You want me to interview you? Usually, that consists of me asking questions and the other person telling the truth."

Carrer folded his hands open. "Ask whatever you like. I have nothing more to hide."

"Why did you kill Florez just now? He did what you asked him to do, and you shot him. You even made damn sure he was dead. Wasn't he a friend of yours?"

Carrer shrugged. "He was a business associate. Yes, he did what I asked him to do and delivered you here. But before that, he betrayed me. I do not take kindly to people betraying me, Miss King."

"Is that why you killed Chloe Wilcox and, more recently, Maureen Wagner? Do you see it as a betrayal that they wanted to tell someone about what you did to them?"

Carrer gave her an ironic little smile. "And I suppose you see it differently? That's because you're a woman. You think you can just change your mind after making promises, and the world should just fall in love with you."

Hmmm, that wasn't the admission of guilt that Sam was hoping for. If Michael and the rest of them were really listening and recording this, Sam prayed to God that they were. But she knew it still wasn't enough.

"Where is Chloe's body? I always wondered what you did with her after you killed her that night. You know, her poor sister is still wondering what happened to her."

Carrer burst out laughing. He saw Sam looking at him as if he had lost his mind. "I'm sorry. Of course, you don't yet understand the irony of asking that. Chloe is where you'll be ending up, too, eventually, after I'm done with you."

Carrer pointed his finger to the window. Sam looked and saw the woods on the outskirts of the property. "There's a nice little patch of ground there with your name on it. You'll be taking your eternal rest next to little Chloe Wilcox. Poetic justice, I think, since it's your fault she's dead. If you hadn't put the idea in her head that you could somehow save her... but never mind. It's also poetic to finish this where it all started."

"What do you mean where it all started?" Sam asked. She felt a flutter in her stomach telling her she was edging closer to some truth about Carrer—some dark truth that would make the man himself finally make sense.

"This house. My maternal grandparents. They were the ones who showed me that there was a difference between us and the rest of the world. Some people are born into power, Miss King. They are the main characters, and the story of life is about them. There are only a handful of us, and taking what we want from the rest of the world, that is our birthright."

What a twisted way of looking at the world, Sam thought.

"I admire you for striving to be one of the key players, by the way. You certainly strove for your life to matter. In the end, though, you'll see that you don't mean all that much."

Sam ignored this statement, delivered so matter-of-factly. Instead, she asked Carrer, "How exactly did your grandparents teach you this? Did they abuse you like you abused all those girls?"

Carrer shook his head. "That's a very naive way of thinking. You think I was abused, and thus, there's a simple explanation for why I choose to live a certain way. No, Miss King. My grandfather brought people home for the three of us to play with. Men, women—my grandparents didn't have a preference. They were usually prostitutes or homeless people. The first time they let me inside the playroom, I was about eight years old. You can't imagine how thrilling it was—how mesmerizing to see the power my grandparents could wield over the ones they chose. In my eyes, my grandparents were gods." Carrer gave that laugh of his again, making the skin on the back of Sam's neck crawl. "I admit, I was very young."

Something in his voice, in the way he said that last bit... "You did something to them, didn't you?"

"Well, they got so old. And rather senile in the end. I wanted their money. As their favorite grandchild, I deserved it. Not those brats my mother had after she walked out on my father. I was the only one they shared their secrets with. Still, I could see it in their eyes when they spoke about their *other grandchildren*. Twins—a girl and a boy. They wanted to leave them something, too. So, I took them to the playroom before they could change their will to include the two brats. I couldn't avoid some of the family fortune going to my useless mother, though."

Samantha did find it interesting that Carrer's entire fortune was built on the murder of his grandparents. She also needed to keep him talking. While he had been relaying his story, he stood up from the couch and walked over to the large window facing the front of the house. It was the same as the interview in his office when he had sat on the windowsill with his back to the world outside, facing Sam as he spoke.

"Didn't the police ever suspect it was you? Or connect the people your grandparents killed with them?"

"I took their bodies to the stables and set them on fire. My grandfather loved smoking cigars, so everybody assumed it was a tragic accident. A few purebred horses died, and others, unfortunately, had to be put down. I felt sorry about that. They were beautiful animals." But Carrer didn't look sorry. He looked away in the distance. He looked nostalgic, and Sam had the impression he was reliving a fond memory. Did he stay to watch the fire burn? Did he enjoy the sound of the suffering animals? Sam thought the answer was yes. He was a sadist, after all.

"As for their playmates, why would anyone ask questions about that? They were both upstanding members of society."

Carrer gave a regretful sigh. "I appreciate you giving me the opportunity to wander down memory lane, Miss King. But I'm afraid we have to get back to the matter at hand."

With his back still turned to the window, his full attention on Sam, he stood up and walked slowly toward her.

A movement outside caught Sam's attention, and she saw the masked face of someone wearing a SWAT uniform glancing in the window. The face disappeared so fast after taking stock of the situation that Sam might have hallucinated it, but the sense of relief that washed over her told her she hadn't.

She glanced back at Carrer, not wanting him to suspect what she knew; that rescue had come after all, and he was but a few seconds away from being arrested.

Time for your final piece of acting, Sam, she thought to herself, *and you better make it good.*

Arranging her face into a look of absolute terror, Sam shied away from Carrer. "Please! Please don't! Don't take me to your grandparents' playroom! I'll do anything, but please don't take me there!"

She could see that Carrer was enjoying her fear. He was enjoying watching her beg. He was so enraptured by it that he forgot all about the gun in his pocket. If he had remembered about the gun, the next few seconds could have ended horribly, with him shooting Sam.

Instead, at the crucial moment when the SWAT team threw a flash grenade through the window, Sam recognized it for what it was. She sank out of the chair and onto the floor, crawling across the carpet until she had the larger couch as cover. Then, she had her hands over her ears, pinching her eyes shut and waiting for the chaos to descend on them.

Carrer looked stupidly down at the flash grenade and was caught completely by surprise when it went off with an enormous, world-shattering bang.

Chapter 18:

Revelations and Rescue

Sam lifted her head up and, through the smoke, could see policemen dressed all in black swarming inside the room.

She peeked from behind the couch and watched with satisfaction as Carrer was roughly turned over onto his stomach, his hands cuffed behind him. She watched his face as he was dragged outside, a member of the SWAT team on either side.

Through his coughing and his streaming eyes, he spotted Samantha crouched down behind the couch. A look of manic hate passed over his face, and he lunged at her, but the policemen grabbed him and escorted him past Sam.

"Miss King?... Miss King? Is there anyone else inside the house?"

Sam looked up at the policeman leaning over her. She shook her head, then remembered Carrer's two henchmen that she hadn't seen since they had taken Florez's body away. "There were two other guys that worked for Carrer. Bodyguard types. They took Emilio Florez away, and I don't know where they went. Florez was dead. Carrer shot him."

“We have them in custody, Miss King.”

The policeman held one hand out to Sam and helped her up. “Are you hurt?”

Sam shook her head. She couldn’t believe that she had actually gotten out of this without a scratch. The policeman escorted her outside, where she immediately saw Michael, looking sick with worry, bobbing up and down on his heels to see when Sam was brought out. When he saw her, a look of relief washed over his gruffly handsome face.

He met her halfway and folded her in an enormous hug. “God, Sam, I thought he was going to kill you at any second before we had a chance to mobilize a rescue team.”

Sam pulled away and looked up at Michael. “You were listening on the hidden recorder? You heard what he told me?”

He nodded. “Yeah, we heard everything. As soon as Tony and I realized where you had gone, we went to Florez’s room, but he had already taken you. I suspected he was taking you to Carrer, so I logged in through the app. Of course, it wasn’t recording yet because you hadn’t turned it on at your end. I tried to get a SWAT team together, in case you had a chance to switch it on, and we could trace your location. The police were resistant at first, saying there wasn’t enough evidence that you were kidnapped. Even when the audio started coming in, and Carrer mentioned where he had you, they said it could be a publicity stunt. That's when Janice Lockland stepped in. She got the news station to broadcast the audio feed live. Everyone heard what Carrer told you, and some bureaucratic heads are going to roll because of this."

Michael led Sam to the ambulance. "Come on, they're taking you to the hospital to check you out. You've just suffered a very traumatic experience."

For once, Sam didn't argue but lay back quietly on the stretcher. She closed her eyes when the ambulance drove away from the hellhole where Carrer had buried his last victims. She could feel Michael's hand and was relieved to have him there with her.

The doctor determined that Sam was physically unharmed and that she could go home. He did, however, suggest that she take it easy over the next few days. Michael took her back to his house. She had a shower while he cooked them a simple meal.

After Sam ate, she was exhausted. Michael took her to the main bedroom, where she stretched out on the comfy bed. When he covered her with a blanket, Sam thought how nice it was to be taken care of for once. Her eyes were closed, and she was already drifting away.

***

Sam came awake with a start. For a few seconds, she didn't know where she was and thought she was back in the suitcase, in the trunk of Florez's car, being taken to Carrer. When the memories crashed back in all at once, Sam felt around in the dark room for the bedside lamp. She found the switch and relaxed when the welcome light flooded the room.

Taking a sweatshirt from Michael's closet, she stepped into the living room and saw him emptying a bag onto the coffee table. "I got you a burner phone. Yours has unfortunately gone into evidence. They found it on one of Carrer's goons. You need a phone, so I thought you could use that one until you got yourself sorted with a proper one."

Sam took the phone gratefully and kissed Michael on the cheek. "Thank you." Both of them understood that she was thanking him for more than just the cell phone. She had seen her bags standing in one corner of the living room and knew that Michael had gone to the hotel to fetch her things. He understood that Sam couldn't be alone just then, not after her latest ordeal, and had volunteered his place as a base of operations and a place to live without there having to be a discussion about it. This take-charge attitude may have been annoying to Sam, who had always been so independent, but Michael was the exception.

They understood each other, and that kind of connection was rare.

"You'll have to give a statement tomorrow. I'll take you to the station myself. That's the longest I can stall them, I'm afraid."

Sam nodded and was grateful that she had until the next day to give her statement to the police.

"Janice called a few times while you were asleep. She's desperate to reschedule the interview."

Sam laughed. "I'm so sorry that you were forced to be my assistant while I was asleep."

Michael came over and took her in his arms. "I don't mind. I do hope you'll forgive me, though, when you hear what I agreed to. Tony is throwing you a victory party at the *Monkey Loft*. He booked a private room and everything."

Sam groaned, but even as she did, she understood why it would be good for her to let her hair down, have a few drinks, and spend a good time with people she knew.

"Well, I better go get ready, then. Tony can be quite pushy when he wants to be. Especially about social obligations."

A few hours later, when they walked inside the private room at the *Monkey Loft*, Sam felt slightly overwhelmed by the sea of faces toasting her. She spotted Tony sitting at a table with Dana Anderson and Dylan Summers. She and Michael made their way over, stopping here and there so Sam could accept praise for how she handled one of the biggest stories *The Seattle Telegraph* had ever seen. Sam realized that they were congratulating her for still being alive when Carrer had done everything in his power to silence her.

Just as they sat down and Sam accepted a flute of champagne, she spotted a familiar face in the crowd. A young man was standing against the wall, watching her and the rest of them. He looked like he wanted to say something to Sam but was too shy to come over. Sam put her drink down and walked over to where Kyle Brenner was standing.

When he saw Sam, he gave a sad little smile.

"Hey, it's good to see you. This is a surprise! What on earth are you doing here?"

Kyle shrugged. "I've actually been back in Seattle for a few weeks. I left Ryan. He confessed what he did, taking the money from Carrer to give up where we were living. I'm so sorry I left, Sam. I regretted it from the moment we set foot in Argentina."

"It's okay. You got scared. It happens."

Kyle shook his head. "It didn't happen to you, or at least you didn't let being scared stop you. I've been begging Tony to take me back, but I guess he felt that I needed to make amends with you."

Samantha turned around and looked over at Tony, who was watching her and Kyle. She turned back to her old assistant. "Consider your apology accepted. I'll be glad to have you back."

Sam and Kyle were making their way back to the table when a man came up to them. He was young, perhaps 25 years old, with long blond hair tied back in a ponytail. Sam saw the flushed look on his face and the deranged anger in his eyes. Kyle saw it, too, and realized what the madman's intention was before Sam did.

Kyle pushed Sam out of the way as the guy was crashing into them. He enveloped the guy in a hug and swept his feet out from under him in one fluid motion. The stranger fell down onto the floor, and as he did, the knife he had been carrying—intended for Sam—went clattering across the floor.

Kyle was sitting on top of the guy as he screamed abuse in Sam's direction, his blond hair flailing, spittle flying from his shouting mouth. Some people screamed when they realized what had almost happened, but for the most part, everyone just stood around in shock, watching this development.

“You bitch!” Sam heard the madman yell. “You should die for what you did! Carrer is a good man! How dare you dirty his name like that?”

Eventually, security came and dragged the man outside, but the damage was done, putting a damper on Tony’s party. The police were called, and everyone present was asked to give a statement.

Afterward, Sam caught up with Kyle in the parking lot. He was about to climb into his car. Sam hugged him tightly. “You saved my life. So, if it wasn’t clear before, I want to see you at your old desk first thing Monday morning.”

She laughed as Kyle gave her a little salute, and she watched him drive off into the evening traffic.

Michael caught up with Sam outside the club. “Seems like your party is a bust. We can go back inside if you want and have a drink or two.”

Sam shook her head. “No, thanks. I’d rather just go home with you.”

Michael smiled and put his arm around Sam’s neck. They turned around and made their way to the car. “I was hoping you would say that.”

Chapter 19:

Aftermath and Truth

Sam could feel the bright studio lights beating down on her like so many suns. She felt their glare, and the nervous fluttering in her middle increased tenfold.

When she had finally set a date for this one-on-one interview with Janice Lockland, it had seemed very far into the future. Now, it was there, the moment when she would be telling the world how a senator and a supreme court judge were also involved in Carrer's inner circle.

"It's good to finally have you here with us in the studio, Miss King."

"Please, call me Sam." she smiled at Janice, and suddenly, her nervousness melted away. She wasn't used to being in the spotlight like this. She usually told her stories from behind her computer screen. Sam supposed it was as good a chance as any to prepare herself for the moment when she would have to go on the stand and testify how Carrer had killed Emilio Florez in front of her and the things he had confessed. She had received a deposition to testify only the day before. Carrer's trial was gaining massive media attention, and there were bound to be news cameras present.

"Of course. As the woman who singlehandedly brought the terrible truth of Colmbs Carrer's musical empire to the surface and shed light on the corruption of so many people involved in his inner circle, what would you like to tell the people watching today?"

"Firstly, and most importantly, I would like to point out that it wasn't a story that ever would have been told if I had done so single-handedly. If not for the remarkable courage of all the victims who have stepped forward and said, 'This is what happened to me,' then the story would have remained dead. So, to each and every victim going to testify against Carrer, I would like to say thank you. Your testimonies will certainly mean an end to this particular organization's dirty work."

"Your last explosive interview with Carrer nearly cost you your life. It was, in fact, broadcast live on our very own news station. Yet some experts have claimed that the recorded audio file may be deemed inadmissible as evidence and that you yourself, in fact, may be facing charges because Carrer was unaware that your conversation was being recorded. It is illegal to record a conversation without the person's knowledge, I understand. Are you afraid you'll be facing charges because of it?"

"It's rather a gray area, and I have to see what the police, the state prosecutor, and Carrer's own legal team decide, but I'm not afraid that charges will be brought forward. If you'll recall, I did ask Carrer if he wanted me to interview him, if he was willing to tell me the truth. He agreed to the interview. The fact that he was unaware of the recording, that the interview was being broadcast over national television, doesn't change the fact that police found evidence at the house of Carrer's grandparents to support the idea that he was, in fact, telling the truth. One of the bodies discovered on the grounds was that of Chloe Wilcox, who had been missing for many months. Her sister finally got to bury her. It should be noted that at the time I was conducting the interview with Carrer, I wasn't aware that the broadcast was going out live either. My only motivation was to survive, to get out of there alive, and for Carrer to pay for what he did."

"Chloe's body wasn't the only one found on the grounds. Shortly before your interview with Carrer, the fashion photographer Emilio Florez was also killed by Carrer. What was his involvement in the human trafficking ring?"

"Florez came to me shortly after I confronted Louise Sutton with her involvement in the human trafficking ring. If you can recall, both Colmbs Carrer and Wayland Scott had broken ties with Florez very publicly, crippling his image and basically leaving him out to dry. I think Carrer saw the writing on the wall and wanted to set Florez up as a scapegoat in the minds of the public.

Florez provided me with crucial information that helped me identify other sources and gather more evidence. Emilio Florez was crucial in bringing Carrer and Scott down. For him, it was largely motivated by revenge. In the end, he sold me out. He was, of course, the one who kidnapped me and took me to Carrer. Unfortunately for Florez, Carrer didn't forgive his betrayal so easily. I was there when Carrer shot him. It was done very quickly, in cold blood, and Carrer definitely wanted to be sure that Florez was dead."

"By now, everyone has heard that the tragic suicide of Wayland Scott came about after you exposed him as being involved in this sex trafficking ring. Do you regret naming him as one of the perpetrators?"

Samantha thought carefully about how she wanted to phrase her answer. Wayland Scott had been a beloved music producer. His charming and magnetic personality ensured he still had a lot of fans. Some of them were reluctant to believe he had been involved in anything so horrifying.

Sam decided, though, that the memory of Wayland Scott and what people wanted to believe about him weren't more important than the truth.

"It is a tragedy that Wayland Scott will not be held accountable for his actions in a court of law. I do not regret that I told the truth in my preliminary report. The state prosecutor has all the evidence that I have, and I am sure the extent of Scott's involvement and the exact nature of his own crimes will come as a shock to his friends and family. I am not without sympathy for the loved ones he left behind, who will be forced to live under the shadow of the crimes he committed. I do, however, feel telling the truth is important. That's why I came on your show—because there is still a truth to be told."

"You've hinted before at the involvement of two powerful men that you have not revealed the names of in your preliminary report. Are you saying you are ready to divulge those names now for all the viewers to hear?"

"I am. I'd like to make it clear that the police and the state prosecutor have those names as well, but as of yet, both of these men are still walking free. They haven't even been brought in for questioning, let alone been arrested, and there is ample evidence to prove their involvement in the human trafficking ring. Both men profited from their business dealings with Colmbs Carrer, and I think the public has a right to ask why nothing has been done to put these two men behind bars."

Janice leaned forward, obviously eager to hear the names of the two powerful men. "So, who is it?"

"It's State Senator Andrew Torres and Supreme Court Judge Nicolai Salomon."

Pandemonium erupted in the studio as no one, not even those professional people connected to the news station, could keep their cool. The scandal was way too shocking, as Samantha knew it would be.

Janice called for a short commercial break, and she turned to Sam. "We have about 10 minutes, so come on."

The tall, red-headed woman with the dangerous green cobra eyes led Sam outside the building. They walked onto a small balcony that looked out over the gardens. With a shaky hand, Janice opened her handbag and took out a cigarette. She offered one to Sam, who declined the offer. Janice lit her cigarette and, after a few excited puffs, turned to Sam.

"My God, that was brilliant! You have some balls."

Sam laughed, remembering those had been Tony's exact words to her a few times. "Yeah, I've heard that before."

"I know you're holding most of it back for your expose, but do you have proof here of Salomon and Torres's involvement? Anything will do. Otherwise, both of us are bound to be stoned to death when we next go out in public."

Sam knew the public would have a very strong opinion about her accusation. Torres was an ex-minister, and Salomon actually ran a nonprofit that had always claimed its goal was to abolish the human trafficking trade.

Sam handed Janice a memory stick. Janice looked at it for a moment and then at Sam with one eyebrow raised. "This is security footage of the two men meeting Carrer in a Seattle shipping yard. Behind them, you can see men with guns escorting frightened young women onto a shipping container. There's also a shot of an envelope exchanging hands. My guess would be money, of course."

Janice took the memory stick with an incredulous look on her face. "The police, the state prosecutor... do you mean they have this? The men's faces are clear in the video?"

Sam nodded quietly.

"I can see why you brought it here, why it was so important to make this public. You're afraid the state prosecutor is going to bury this, aren't you? Along with the police?"

Sam didn't have to think about it. "Yes, that's what I'm afraid of. I think Carrer's whole operation can, in fact, be traced back to Christoph Berger. In the very beginning, when I started my investigation, I saw a photo in Carrer's office of him and Berger in front of Carrer's nightclub,

Persephone. What if the prosecutor who had tried Berger's case had evidence of either Torres or Salomon's involvement back then? Maybe even Carrer's? I think they did. My gut tells me they did, and they buried it because the scandal would have been too huge."

"So, you're hoping that by revealing these names, this will have a ripple effect and expose the whole thing, top to bottom?" There was a definite note of admiration in Janice's voice. She and Sam had now found that brief but strong sense of camaraderie that those in their profession experience when discussing an explosive, interesting, and, in this case, word-shattering story. Janice was a little jealous that it wasn't her story, but she was also raring to be part of it and to help Sam in any way she could.

Sam nodded. "That's what I'm hoping for, yes. Shake a tree violently enough; you'll get almost all the fruit from the bottom branches, and that's great. If you keep going, though, some of the fruit at the top is bound to come tumbling down, too."

Janice laughed and put out her cigarette. Their 10 minutes were more than up; it was time to go.

She opened the door to let Sam walk through. "Good for you! Now, let's see if I can help you shake the hell out of that tree."

Later, as Sam was driving back to the hotel room where NBC Washington had once again footed the bill for Sam to stay while she was there for the interview, Sam reflected on the reaction of the public and the scrutiny she herself was bound to face because of it. It wasn't over yet. There was still Carrer's trial to get through, and Sam was now sure that Torrez and Salomon would be facing legal charges as well. It had been a crazy ten months since Kyle first told her the story.

Kyle, back at *The Telegraph* offices where he belonged, had met a nice twenty-something attorney, and the two of them were talking of moving in together.

Sam herself was already missing Michael and looking forward to going home. They had decided to make living arrangements for Sam to live with Michael permanently. It worked so well for them, and their lives fit in with each other's so perfectly that their relationship felt much longer than it really had been.

Sam parked her car in front of the Fairmont Hotel and handed her keys to the valet. Her phone was on silent. All she wanted right then was to call Michael and get his impression of the interview she had just given, to wish him a good night, to have a nice long bath, and to order room service.

Chapter 20:

The Final Note

Sam was just finishing her last bit of coffee when Michael gave her a peck on the cheek. As she held the side of his face in her left hand, her engagement ring, given a few weeks before, sparkled prettily.

Michael handed her a piece of paper:

Be at this address around ten-thirty this morning. There's something I want to show you.

Sam looked at the address but couldn't tell what type of place it was for. "Ooh, mysterious! Okay, I'll play along. Have a good day, babe."

After her shower, with her wet, dark-blond hair tied back in a clip, Sam made her way to the office of *The Seattle Telegraph.* Following Carrer's trial and her expose, Sam had gotten more than a few offers from papers and news stations all across Washington, desperate to snatch her up. The most tempting of these had come from NBC Washington, where Sam would have worked side-by-side with Janice Lockland.

In the end, though, Sam had decided she wanted the craziness to settle down, not gear up. She wanted to be part of a paper that would focus on other stories as well, not just the one that had made her famous.

For the first time in her life, she had found something that was easily as important as her career, and she wanted to see where that would take her. She knew if she started swimming in a bigger fish tank, the job would consume her every waking moment, and there wouldn't be time for anything else.

Swiping her security card, Sam took the elevator to the familiar old floor. Same building, same people, but Sam had a brand-new office. Five months before, her beloved boss, Tony Prescott, had passed away from a heart attack. It hadn't taken long for the top brass of the paper to offer Samantha the position of Editor in Chief.

She had to push her guilt aside because even Tony's wife assured Sam that it was what Tony would have wanted. Her guilt had only been part of it. She found that she desperately wanted the job; she knew she could do it and that it was something she would be good at. She was right. Three months in, she was comfortable in her new position, and the paper was doing well.

As she pushed the door to the newsroom open and made her way to Tony's old office, there were a few calls of "Morning, Boss!" that greeted her as she walked past. Her name was etched on the door, and seeing that, Sam felt the familiar twinge of pride that would probably fade over time. What she hoped wouldn't fade was the faint whiff of tobacco from Tony's beloved cigars that still clung to every surface of the office. It was like the ghost of it was a reminder that he would always be there in spirit if she needed him.

Her faint smile turned to a frown of concentration as she sat behind her computer and dove into work. Minutes flew by. Sam was just catching up on a bit of correspondence when there was a knock on her open door.

Leaning back in her chair, Sam smiled when she saw Kyle Brenner with two cups of coffee in his hands. She took one of the offered coffees gratefully but frowned at him playfully. "What did I tell you about this? You're not my assistant anymore, so you shouldn't be bringing me coffee. We don't pay you those extra bucks as a reporter for you to carry people's coffee around."

He waved at her dismissively. "Maybe I'm just brownnosing my way to another promotion."

"So, how's the Winters girl working out so far?" She was referring to Becky Winters, Kyle's newly appointed young assistant.

Kyle shrugged. "A bit dewy-eyed, but that won't last, as we both know."

Sam grinned. "Yeah, we were all young and innocent once."

“She’s hungry, though, and very clever. I think she’ll be fine.”

Sam drummed her fingers on her desk, wondering not only about Becky being ready for a top assignment but also about Kyle, too. “Think she’s ready to dip a toe in the deep end?”

Kyle looked at Sam quizzically. She took a deep breath before replying, “Carrer agreed to an interview. As you know, it’s the first time since Torrez and Salomon were incarcerated at the D.C. Central Penitentiary that any of them have agreed to an interview. I want you to do it and to take Winters along as your assistant. If Carrer makes rude comments to her, then we’ll know that he’s not serious about the interview. Don’t let him drag it out. Show him who’s in charge and show that you’re willing to walk away if he doesn’t play nice.”

“Are you sure, Sam? This is your story.” Even as Kyle said it, Sam could see he was eager to do it. She knew in her gut that she was making the right call. As an investigative journalist, it was important to have that killer instinct—to fight for your story and to chase it down at almost any cost. As the Editor in Chief, though, her job was no longer to steal the limelight but to delegate and lead others to find the right stories. It was time for her to let go. She herself had gotten all she personally could from Carrer, and it was no longer in her best interest to hold on to it or feel possessive about the story.

"Get out of here. I have work to do, you know. Let me know how it went."

She had the pleasure of seeing Kyle leave her office floating on a cloud of excitement at the prospect of interviewing Carrer.

A notification on her phone chimed, reminding her that she needed to leave if she was to be at the address Michael had given her at the time he had specified. She was curious to see what his surprise was. Though he wasn't averse to arranging a romantic surprise now and then, it definitely wasn't something he did too often, which, of course, made the times he did it that much more special.

Sam had a feeling, though, that this surprise wasn't meant to be romantic. It was something else, and the fact that she couldn't begin to imagine what it was made it that much more intriguing.

"What the hell?" Sam loudly wondered when she saw that the GPS had taken her to the airport. She uneasily wondered if Michael had gone mad and arranged a trip for them. In that case, she would have to disappoint him because she couldn't leave. She was only three months into her new job. After she had parked her car and headed inside, she called Michael and told him where she was. She saw him a few moments later riding down the escalator with a big grin on his face, clearly enjoying her consternation.

When they met up, Michael gave her a quick kiss. "Come on, you're just in time." He led Sam to a section of the airport reserved for smaller, private planes. Here, a few people were standing around in the waiting area. Sam looked around, noticing the people's faces were all set in various degrees of eagerness, anticipation, anxiety, and fear. It was clear that some of the people knew each other, and these stood around in close little bundles. It dawned on Sam that those standing together were little families in most cases but that they were strangers to the rest of the people.

Michael leaned over and whispered to Sam, "No press was invited for this occasion. There will be a press release a few days from now, but it's important to give them their privacy for this one moment."

Sam wanted to ask what she was doing there, but she decided to just let it play out. While she waited for whatever it was that was supposed to happen, she noticed a young man standing with an older man and a woman, waiting anxiously. The young man looked vaguely familiar, and it scratched at the back of Sam's mind. She felt like she almost had it; she knew this young man. Then, her attention was drawn away as someone pointed out a small plane that had just landed.

Near-hysterical excitement swept across the waiting crowd, and Sam watched their reaction with awe.

One of the women walked over to the door, where a kindly security guard reminded her that she couldn't walk down the runway. The woman went to the window instead, where everyone, besides Michael and Sam, was crowding around for a better look.

"There is she! I see her! That's Brenda!" Sam made out the excited yell of one older woman in the cacophony of excited voices, all talking over each other.

It finally dawned on Sam what was happening when she saw the woman burst into tears. It was the tears of utter joy, relief, and sorrow. Sam recognized the name. Brenda Victor had been just shy of her sixteenth birthday when she disappeared. Sold to an overseas buyer by Carrer and his associates, she had spent the better part of three years in the clutches of her buyer in Western Germany.

"How... when..." was all Sam could get out. Her knees were feeling weak suddenly. Michael led her to one of the seats against the wall. It was sufficiently far away from the crowd so he and Sam could talk.

"Of the fifty girls we have so far identified as being victims of Carrer's human trafficking ring, we've managed to track down ten of them. The buyers have been arrested, and this is only the first batch of girls we managed to extradite from foreign countries back to the USA. In the following months, there will be more, I'm sure of it."

Sam looked back at the families and realized where she had seen the young man before. It was Maxine Wilson's boyfriend. The young man had never given up his fight for Maxine. Sam had spoken to him briefly at the beginning of her investigation, had interviewed him regarding Maxine, and had seen him being interviewed on other news stations since.

"So, Maxine Wilson, she's..." For the first time in her life, Sam couldn't find the words to string a coherent sentence together. What she was feeling inside drowned out and pushed out everything else.

"See for yourself," Michael said quietly.

Sam watched as the doors opened and girls, looking thin, even dirty in most cases, made their way inside and were enveloped in hugs, their faces covered with kisses by loved ones who had, in some cases, given up hope of ever seeing them alive again.

Sam immediately recognized Maxine Wilson, though the girl with tears streaming down her cheeks was a far cry from the pretty, vivacious young girl she had been almost two years before.

This girl... Sam could see by the haunted look in her eye that she may never again be the same. Whatever she had experienced had been brutal and unthinkable. Still, she had survived and, with the support of her loving family and friends, would continue surviving her unthinkable ordeal.

Next to Sam, Michael cleared his throat, and Sam could see her reaction to this emotion-filled reunion reflected in his eyes.

"I thought it was important to show you why all those sacrifices you made were necessary. Why it was so important, and why it was so amazing what you did. I love you."

Again, Sam couldn't find the words to tell him what this gift meant to her. She picked up his hand and kissed the back of it. Then, they watched the reunion for a few minutes more. Sam knew that soon, she and Michael would leave these people alone to pick up the broken pieces of their lives that were so tragically interrupted.

For now, she was content to just bask in their joy and feel the grateful joy in her own heart.

www.ingramcontent.com/pod-product-compliance
Lightning Source LLC
La Vergne TN
LVHW041212150826
845673LV00001B/372

* 9 7 8 1 8 3 6 6 3 4 5 1 5 *